# London Loves

Theresa Troutman

# DEDICATION

This book is dedicated to every reader who took this journey with me and joined Sebastian and Tess on their adventure. May your lives be filled with love, loyalty and laughter!

Thank you for taking time to read the books in the Love's Great Adventure Series. If you enjoyed them, please consider telling your friends or posting a short review. Word of mouth is an author's best friend and much appreciated.

Summer 1991

# Chapter 1 - Something So Strong

Tess walked into the condo to the smell of chicken roasting in the oven. She found Sebastian sitting on the sofa with Mattie, reading a children's book. "Hey, you two," she greeted, dropping her briefcase on the floor.

"Mummy!" Mattie exclaimed, jumping off the couch and running to hug her mom.

Kneeling down to Mattie's eye level, she asked, "How was your day?"

"Great! Daddy is teaching me to read."

"I hope he's starting you out with something good."

Sebastian walked over and kissed Tess on the cheek. "Just something light—*War and Peace.*"

Tess laughed aloud while Mattie cocked her head and gave her a confused look. "What's so funny?"

"Daddy made a joke."

"It wasn't funny," Mattie replied. She ran back to the sofa and grabbed her book, picking it up to show Tess the cover. It was Dr. Seuss' *One Fish, Two Fish, Red Fish, Blue Fish.*

"You're starting her off with poetry?"

"Well, it's not Keats."

"She's four years old, Bas. Cut her some slack," Tess chided.

"Ah, this from the valedictorian of St. Alexander's High School and graduate of NYU with honors."

"I'm going to change," Tess said, ignoring his comment.

"Dinner will be ready in fifteen minutes." Sebastian turned to his daughter. "Mattie, go wash your hands before we eat."

After dinner, they tucked Mattie into bed and Sebastian read her a bedtime story: *A Bear Called Paddington.* At least he tried to read her the story, but Mattie kept interrupting.

"Do bears really like marmalade?" she asked.

"I don't see why not. The next time I run into one, I'll ask him."

Mattie giggled. "Daddy, where are you going to run into a bear in New York?"

"The Central Park Zoo."

"Oh, yeah," Mattie agreed, nodding her head.

"Your daddy used to live in London a long time ago," Tess added.

"Have you been to Paddington Station?" Mattie asked, her eyes wide with excitement.

"Yes, I have."

"I want to go! Maybe we can find Paddington Bear there."

Sebastian glanced over at Tess with a look that said *see what you started?* Tess simply smiled and took a seat in Sebastian's lap. "I want to go, too," she chimed in.

"Enough for tonight—time for bed." He closed the book and set it on Mattie's bedside table. Then he leaned over and kissed his little girl. "Love you, darling."

"'Night, Mattie," Tess said, also giving her daughter a kiss.

Sebastian turned off the light. He and Tess left the room before he closed the bedroom door.

It was blissfully quiet once Mattie fell to sleep. Sebastian and Tess curled up on the couch together, enjoying some time alone. Since graduating NYU, Tess had gotten a job with the Associated Press. Sebastian continued working at Fiona Ashford

Gallery in Chelsea on a part-time basis while raising Mattie. They had settled into a happy, calm existence. It was a welcome change of pace for the couple. The first few years living together had certainly been bumpy, but they'd survived and become stronger people for it. Now they both had everything they'd ever wanted.

"Sooooo…I have some big news," Tess announced, looking up at her husband.

"What?"

"The AP offered me a position in London!" Tess said, bursting with excitement.

"Really? So soon? You've only worked there for a few years."

"I know, but I was talking with my boss. I told him that you're English and you keep up on the current news trends going on over there. He thought I'd be the perfect person for the position."

"Because you have an 'in' with me?" Sebastian chuckled. "See, I told you it's always who you know that matters in life. I just never thought I'd be talking about myself."

"I don't care if you were the one that tipped the job in my favor, I want to do it. What do you think? Can we move to London?"

Sebastian held Tess in his arms and pondered what she had just asked of him. He knew it was a dream of his wife's to travel the world and work as a journalist. He couldn't deny her the opportunity. He was just surprised that it was London and not some other European city. Sebastian did miss his homeland, and he thought of all the fun he could have showing his daughter around town. "I say we do it."

Tess gave him a big, toothy grin. "Thank you! I love you!"

"When do they want you to move?"

"In a month. I told them I would need to make a trip over to find a place to live first. I had a video conference with the London office and they said they'd help us set everything up. Just imagine—we'll be able to see Penny and Sigourney more often." Sigourney had moved back to London for a position in the London Symphony Orchestra, and Sebastian did miss being able to see her.

"Then I'll book the tickets. Mattie's going to love this!"

Sebastian walked into the Fiona Ashford Gallery the next day, excited about his family's upcoming move overseas. Fiona waved as she finished up business on the phone.

"Fiona, how are you?"

"Fine, how are you? You're not scheduled today."

"Can we talk?"

"I don't like tone of your voice," Fiona said as she sat on the leather sofa.

"Tess was offered a job in London. I was hoping you'd let me transfer to the gallery over there."

Fiona sighed with relief. "Thank goodness, I thought you were going to quit. I would love for you take a position in the London gallery. Your connections with the art world over there should get the gallery off the ground. Honestly, it's been exhausting for me to fly back and forth all the time. I'll even bump up your salary."

"That's a very generous offer, Fiona. Thank you."

"You're welcome. I'm happy that you're going, but I'm certainly going to miss you."

"You should invest in computers: the World Wide Web and email is the wave of the future. It will make it so much easier to stay in touch," Sebastian explained.

"Yes, you're right. I've been putting it off, but I suppose you can't stop progress. Will you help me pick something out before you go?"

"Absolutely!"

When Sebastian arrived home, Alice and Mattie were watching cartoons on TV. He thanked her for keeping an eye on Mattie. Alice, in turn, relayed the message that Tess would be home late from work.

"Daddy, what's for dinner tonight?" Mattie asked, while looking at the TV.

"I don't know, Mattie, I just walked through the front door. Mummy's coming home late. It's just you and me tonight, darling."

Mattie turned around on the sofa and swung her arms over the back to face her daddy. "Let's go out to eat."

Sebastian looked down at his Rolex. It was four thirty in the afternoon. "Okay, but first I have a make a phone call. Give me a half an hour and then I'll take you to McDonald's for a Happy Meal."

"Yay!" Mattie exclaimed, jumping on the sofa.

Sebastian walked over to his daughter. "Don't jump on the sofa. You'll fall and break your arm. Oh, and don't tell Mummy about McDonald's, either, got it?"

"But Daddy, she loves McDonald's!"

"Yes, but this is our little secret," Sebastian warned, placing his index finger over his lips to quiet Mattie.

"You got it, Dude!" Mattie agreed and sat back down on the sofa to resume watching TV.

Sebastian shook his head in dismay. "You watch too many episodes of *Full House*, Mattie."

Sebastian called the airline and made arrangements for his family's flight that next week. Mattie would be so excited when he told her the news—hell, he was excited, too. When he hung up the phone, he fetched their coats and they walked a few blocks over to McDonald's.

They sat at a table near the window. Mattie had a hamburger Happy Meal with milk. Sebastian would stop at the Chinese take-away as they headed back home to pick up dinner for himself and Tess.

"Did you have a good day, Daddy?" Mattie asked after taking a sip of milk through her straw.

"I had a very good day."

"What did you do?"

"I went to the gallery to talk with Fiona. Guess what?"

His daughter looked at him, eager to learn the answer to his question. "What?"

"Mummy and I got new jobs in London. We're going to move. What do you think about that?"

"Where Paddington Bear lives?"

Sebastian chuckled. "Yes, among other things. Are you excited?"

Mattie stood up from her chair and rushed over to Sebastian, throwing her little arms around his waist. "Awesome!"

Tess arrived home around eight thirty, tired but happy. Sebastian kissed her. "I have Chinese from Ming's I can warm up for you."

"Did you the get the vegetable spring rolls I love?"

"And the duck sauce," he confirmed with a wink of his eye.

"You are the best," Tess replied, throwing her arms around his waist and giving him a hug.

Tess changed out of her work clothes while Sebastian heated their dinner.

Sitting at the table, Sebastian said, "I booked the plane tickets and spoke with the real estate agent today. We're all set to go."

"I hope we can find a place as nice as this."

"I'll warn you now, places in London are much smaller than here in America—and more expensive."

"Should we sell the condo? Will we have enough money to buy in London? Maybe we should rent."

"The condo is paid for. I think we should keep it. What if you need to fly back to the AP office here in

New York, or we come home to visit your mom, or me to check in with Fiona at the gallery?"

"Henry and Alice will be here to keep an eye on things," Tess agreed. "You're right, we should keep the condo." She reached over for his hand and squeezed it. "Oh, Bas, I just feel like everything is falling into place for us. I'm so excited about this chapter of our lives."

Sebastian gazed at his beautiful, happy wife. "I can't wait either."

# Chapter 2 - London Calling

They caught the British Airways flight out of JFK Airport Sunday afternoon. Sebastian had opted to stay with Penelope Stanton at her townhouse in Kensington rather than take Sigourney up on her offer to stay with her in Mayfair. The last thing Sebastian needed was an unexpected run-in with Lily. She probably didn't even know he had a child and he was very happy to keep it that way.

Once his family had cleared customs, they hailed a black cab into the city, arriving at Penny's home shortly after nine in the evening. Penny opened the red door of her home with a smile on her face. "Welcome to London."

Sebastian ushered his family into the vestibule. Tess and Penny hugged each other. Sebastian kissed Penny on the cheek, while Mattie looked up with great fascination.

"Penny, this is our daughter, Martha," Sebastian introduced.

"You can call me Mattie," the rambunctious four-year-old said, extending her hand in greeting.

"I'm very pleased to meet you, Mattie," Penny said as she knelt down to greet her.

"Daddy said we could search for Paddington Bear at the train station tomorrow. Would you like to come along?"

"I've seen him about that part of town. I would happy to escort you, Mattie."

The child looked up at her father, her eyes dancing with excitement.

"It's late, you need to go to bed, so we can wake early and start our search."

"Where am I sleeping tonight?" Mattie asked.

"Follow me, I'll show you your rooms," Penny announced.

After they had Mattie changed into her pajamas and tucked into bed, the adults sat in the parlor, enjoying a drink. "I'm so glad you took me up on my offer to stay here. I hardly ever get any company." Penny said, sipping her scotch.

"I'm sorry it was so last minute," Tess apologized. "The offer for the job came out of nowhere and we don't have much time to find a place to live. I'm so grateful you could put us up here. I'd hate to drag Mattie to a hotel."

"Have you seen Lily while making the rounds?" Sebastian inquired with hesitation.

"I heard she was at Ascot, but I didn't see her. We usually bump into one another at Wimbledon, but that's not until next month," Penny replied.

"Are you worried about bumping into her?" Tess asked him with concern as she took his hand.

"A little," he admitted. "I don't want her to know about Mattie."

"Sebastian, London is a big town. I'm sure you're worrying for naught." Penny commented.

"I suppose you're right. We don't travel in the same social circles anymore. We should be safe."

"I did see your brother, Maxwell, at a charity event last month. He's making quite the name for himself since your grandfather died and he became Earl of Sutton," Penny said rather impressed.

"Maybe he'll settle down and marry soon. I'm sure Lily won't let up until an heir is born," Sebastian smirked.

"Yes, he's quite the eligible bachelor at the moment."

"You should marry him—then you'd be my sister-in-law," Tess chimed in.

"Oh, I don't think Lily will approve of me," Penny laughed.

"You dated a prince, why wouldn't you be good enough for an earl?" Tess inquired, somewhat confused by the whole conversation.

"Let's just say, I'm not a big of Lady Lily Irons, either."

"Glad we all agree on that," Sebastian muttered, finishing off his scotch. "We've got a full day tomorrow. Tess, we should head off to bed."

"Goodnight, you two," Penny said. "I'll have breakfast ready at eight thirty."

"Thanks, Pen." Sebastian leaned down and kissed her cheek before taking his wife's hand and heading to the guest room.

The four of them sat around the dining table, eating breakfast.

"Daddy, when can we go to the train station?"

"Mattie, we have to meet with the real estate agent today to find our new home. We can't stay with Aunt Penny forever."

"I like it here! There are pretty pink flowers on by bed."

"I'll buy you a blanket with pink flowers for your new bed when we find our home."

Mattie placed the spoon in her cereal bowl and pouted. Sebastian gave her a warning glance.

Penny couldn't contain her laughter. "Let me take her for the day. This way you and Tess can focus on the house hunt without interruption."

"Where will you take her?" Tess asked.

"We can go to Hamley's, have tea at Harrods…"

"And visit Paddington Station?" Mattie asked, sliding to the edge of her seat.

"Yes, we can even visit Paddington Station."

Sebastian looked to Tess, who nodded her head in approval. "Pen, have you ever watched a four-year-old before?"

"No, how hard could it be? She's perfectly behaved. Let her spend the day with Auntie Pen."

Now Sebastian and Tess chuckled in unison. "Fine. Have a lovely day."

"Are you sure about leaving Mattie with Pen?" Sebastian asked as they sat in the back of the black cab on the way to the real estate office.

"She couldn't do any worse than I did when I first started out," Tess reassured.

"Mattie was a baby. She couldn't talk back then."

"Exactly—and now she can. Her vocabulary skills are off the chart, thanks to being raised by you. I'm sure they'll get into some very in-depth conversations today. I only hope they hit it off so we have a babysitter when you and I need a night out."

"I like how you're thinking, Mrs. Irons," Sebastian agreed before kissing her on the lips.

Since they had talked with the agent prior to their arrival, he knew what type of home they needed and had selected some to fit their criteria. They really didn't have a lot of time to fret over a decision; they needed to procure living arrangements quickly and start packing to have everything shipped over from the States. Tess and Sebastian visited six properties. The London housing market was brisk and the agent advised they take the night to talk it over and get back to him first thing in the morning.

"My head's swimming in a sea of confusion," Tess said wearily as they sat down for a late lunch at Harrods.

"I know, but we said we were going to make the decision today."

"We will," she agreed. "Can we start by eliminating any properties?"

"We should knock out the two in Camden Town. I don't feel completely safe there. I'd be worried about you and Mattie."

"I liked the two near Regent's Park. We can take Mattie there to play and it's near the zoo," Tess explained.

"I liked them, but the prices—two hundred thousand pounds. Are you okay with spending that much? They are smaller than the condo we have back home."

"I know. You warned me about that, but it was still shocking to see. The kitchen was so tiny—and that mini-refrigerator. Are you going to be happy cooking there?"

"I can just go to the market every day and buy fresh food to prepare our meals."

Tess looked back and forth between the two photos of the properties. "I guess it all comes down to the garden. If we take the first floor unit, we gain outdoor space. If we take the third floor unit, we get the view."

"You decide. I like them both," Sebastian said, taking her hand.

"It's so much money."

"I'm twenty-five now. The money Nanny left is ours. We can afford it, and I'm sure the prices will only swell as time goes on. It's a good investment, Tess."

"Let's go with the ground floor unit with the garden."

"Excellent—I'll ring Mr. Hume in the morning and we can stop by the agent's office to let him know our decision before we head home." Penny and Mattie walked over to their table. They were carrying shopping bags from various stores. "Well, what have we here?" Sebastian said, picking Mattie up and setting her on his lap.

"We had a brilliant day," Penny said, taking a seat at the table.

"Were you on your best behavior for Aunt Penny?" Tess asked.

"Yes, Mummy."

"And did you find Paddington Bear today?" Sebastian asked his daughter.

"Not the real one," she replied with a frown. "Only stuffed animals."

Sebastian wasn't exactly sure how to respond to that, so he asked another question. "And what did you buy at Hamley's?" It was the local upscale toy store on Regent Street.

Mattie's face lit up and she grabbed for the bag that Penny had set on the floor. Reaching inside, she pulled out a twelve-inch Steiff teddy bear. "Look, Daddy. He's the baby brother of Charles!"

The mohair bear did resemble Sebastian's own teddy bear. "He certainly does look like Charles. Do you think he'll like having a little brother after all this time?"

"I'm sure he'll love it!"

"What did you name him, Mattie?" Tess asked.

"I'll call him Bas."

"You're naming the bear after *me*?" Sebastian asked.

"Mummy calls you Bas all the time and she loves you," Mattie replied. "I love you, too." She reached up and kissed him on the cheek.

Sebastian shook his head. Mattie was too observant and smart for her own good. She definitely took after Tess in that regard. "Well, you know, Charles has been an 'only bear' for many years. I'm not so sure he'll take kindly to a sibling."

Penny tried to conceal her smile as she watched the two interact. She leaned over and whispered to Tess, "I think that is the most adorable thing I have ever seen. If you would have told me this is how Sebastian's life would have ended up ten years ago, I would have said you were mental."

Tess watched Bas and Mattie as they carried on a conversation about two stuffed animals. This was her family and her life couldn't be better.

# Chapter 3 - No Place Like Home

Three weeks later, most of their belongings were packed in a freight container and sailing across the Atlantic toward their new home in London. They decided to keep the condo and not sublet it. If Tess or Sebastian had to travel back and forth for business, they would need a place to stay. The fact that Henry and Alice lived in the same building also gave them peace of mind that the property would be looked after.

Sebastian spent the last morning in New Jersey sipping his coffee while staring out over the Hudson River. Tess walked up behind him and placed her arm around his waist. "What has you so deep in thought?" she asked.

"I was just remembering the first time we stood in this spot and talked about our future. So much has happened in five years."

"Ready for the next step in our life together?"

Sebastian looked down at his wife and smiled. "Yes, I'm excited. I'm also sad because I didn't think I would become so attached to this place. I'm glad we're keeping the condo. It will be comforting to know it's here waiting for us to return."

"That's very sentimental of you, Bas."

Just then Mattie came running into the room. "Is it time yet?" she asked with excitement, leaning up against Tess' leg.

"Yes, today is the day," Tess confirmed.

"Yippee!" Mattie exclaimed, jumping up and down.

"Come and get dressed. Uncle Henry and Aunt Alice will be here to take us to the airport soon," Tess explained as they walked to Mattie's bedroom.

Sebastian smiled to himself—his two girls, giddy with excitement about their new adventure. He was happy he could give them this life, but even more happy that they were his family.

There was a knock at the front door. "It's open," Sebastian called out as he washed his coffee mug in the sink.

Henry and Alice entered the condo. "Good morning. All set to go?" Henry asked.

"Just waiting on Mattie to get dressed."

Mattie came walking out of her bedroom, holding her teddy bear. She made a beeline for Henry, who scooped her up in his arms and gave her a hug. "I'm going to miss you," he told the little girl.

"You'll just have to come and visit us, Uncle Henry."

"Yes, please say you'll come and visit once we get settle in," Tess agreed.

"We've never been out of the country," Alice revealed. "We can't wait to come and visit."

"But when?" Mattie impatiently asked.

"As soon as we get our passports, okay?" Henry explained.

"Okay, let's go!"

"Henry, can you take Mattie to the car and give Tess and me a moment alone?" Sebastian inquired.

Henry nodded while Alice grabbed Mattie's carry-on. They left the condo, giving Tess and Sebastian some privacy.

Sebastian walked over to Tess and took her in his arms. She looked up at him, her eyes brimming with excitement. He leaned in and kissed her. "I love you, Tess." He grabbed the last carry-on bag and took her hand in his.

"Thank you for doing this for us, Bas."

"Anything for my girls."

They locked up the condo and took the elevator to the garage, where Henry waited to drive them to the airport.

Mattie was becoming an old pro at international travel at the ripe old age of four. Sebastian marveled at her resilience. She was completely unfazed by crowds, long queues of people, and changes in time zones. He was so proud of his little girl.

They followed the same routine as three weeks earlier and took a cab into Kensington. They were staying with Penny again until Sebastian and Tess could get their flat unpacked and safe for Mattie.

"Why can't we live with Aunt Penny?" Mattie asked Sebastian in the cab.

"Because, it's not polite to be a permanent house guest."

"But she doesn't work. She likes the company," Mattie announced.

"Oh, really, did she tell you that?"

"Yes."

"But we have a wonderful flat with a nice garden you can play in. Not to mention, we're near Regent's Park and the zoo."

"I think Aunt Penny is lonely. We should find her a boyfriend," Mattie thoughtfully added.

Sebastian looked to Tess in exasperation. He had no clue how to stop her barrage of questions.

"What type of boyfriend do you think Penny would like?" Tess questioned.

Sebastian rolled his eyes. He wanted Tess' help to squelch the inquiry, not encourage it.

"He should be rich and like to shop," Mattie explained.

"Well, London is full of bachelors, I'm sure we can find her a few candidates."

"What's a candidate?" Mattie asked.

Sebastian chuckled. "Yes, Mummy. What's a candidate?"

"A man who would like to be Penny's boyfriend," Tess replied, not missing a beat.

"When can we start looking?"

"As soon as we are unpacked and moved into the flat."

The next day, Sebastian took the call from the movers. Placing the receiver back on the phone, he said, "They're delivering the container at one o'clock today."

"Right on schedule. If we start with the bedrooms, we can stay in our own place tonight," Tess said, excited by the prospect. "Do you think Penny will mind watching Mattie today?"

"Considering they're upstairs going through Penny's closet right now, I don't think that will be a problem."

"We should go check on her," Tess suggested.

They walked up the staircase and down the hall toward Penny's room. The door was open and Sebastian and Tess stopped to watch what was happening inside. Penny had pulled several dresses out of the closet and spread them out on the bed. A half dozen pairs of designer shoes where neatly stacked on the floor. Mattie sat on the floor looking over the contents of Penny's jewelry box.

"What are you two doing?" Sebastian questioned as he walked into the room.

Mattie stood up from the floor and rushed to Sebastian's side. "I'm helping Aunt Penny pick out a dress for the ball."

"So what did you decide?" Tess asked.

Mattie walked over to the black silk Chanel evening gown and pointed to her choice.

"She has great taste," Penny agreed. "We're going with the Chanel. Thank you for your help, Mattie."

"You're welcome. You should wear these shoes," she added, picking up a pair of leather pumps decorated with crystals. She walked back over to her father and said, "Daddy, can you buy me a Chanel dress?"

"Darling, you're four years old. Where are you going to wear it? You have to wear a uniform for school in the fall and your mother and I won't be throwing dinner parties anytime soon."

She gave a pout and it tugged at Sebastian's heart.

"I'll tell you what: when you're sixteen, I'll buy you Chanel." Then he added an additional caveat: "As long as you keep your grades up."

"Well, that shouldn't be a problem since she takes after me. He didn't buy me my first Chanel until I was eighteen," Tess said in mock horror.

Sebastian laughed. "That's not fair, Tess. I didn't know you when you were sixteen."

"I want to see your Chanel!" Mattie exclaimed. "Can I try it on?"

"Once we unpack, you can try it on," Tess agreed.

"Penny, the movers are arriving today. Do you mind watching Mattie until we can get her bedroom sorted out?"

"No problem. She's a joy to have around."

"Can we have tea at Harrods?" Mattie asked.

"Yes, that's an excellent idea. You've been a huge help to me today, Mattie."

"It's settled then. Give us hug," Sebastian said, kneeling down in front of his daughter.

"Do you want to ring me when you're ready for Mattie?"

"Yes, that sounds perfect. Thanks, Penny."

Mattie opened the door to their new flat and raced inside. Sebastian and Tess were bent over boxes, unpacking the kitchen. "Hi, Daddy," she said jumping onto Sebastian's back. He teetered a moment, thrown off balance, but steadied himself to prevent falling over.

"Whoa, what's this all about?" he asked, laughing.

Penny followed behind, setting her purse on the counter. "How are you making out?"

"Mattie, your room is unpacked. Do you want to see it?" Tess asked.

She furiously nodded her head up and down and reached for her mom's hand. The two of them disappeared from the kitchen, leaving Sebastian and Penny alone. "I hope she wasn't too much trouble for you."

"I adore her, Sebastian. I still can't believe you have a child."

"Marrying Tess and having Mattie was the best decisions I ever made. You should try it," he said as his lip curled upwards into a grin.

"Yes, but there is only one problem: in order to get married, I need a boyfriend first." Penny sat at the kitchen table, looking sad and dejected. "Don't suppose you know anyone you'd like to introduce me to?"

"Considering I just moved back, give me a few weeks."

"I'm not getting any younger. I really do think I'd like to settle down and have children."

"You can borrow my precocious four-year-old anytime you'd like," Sebastian offered.

"I'll take you up on that." Penny rose from the chair and kissed Sebastian on the cheek. "I'd best be getting home to prepare for the charity gala. Let me say goodbye to Tess and Mattie."

They walked down the hallway and entered Mattie's room to find Tess and Mattie sitting on the bed talking.

"So what do you think of your new room?" Sebastian asked. The room was a simple square shape. They'd furnished it will a twin-sized bed, a wardrobe, a toy chest, and Mattie's rocking chair. The walls were painted pale pink.

"I love it!"

"I have to get ready for the ball, Mattie. I'll see you later, all right?"

"Can you take pictures, so I can see them later?"

"I'll see what I can do."

"Maybe you'll meet a prince and get married."

Penny gave Sebastian a wary glance. Marrying a prince wasn't in the cards for Penny, she'd had her chance years ago, but it wasn't meant to be. She smiled at Mattie and gave her hug. "You never know what the future holds."

After Mattie was tucked into bed and sleeping, Sebastian and Tess opened a bottle wine and crashed on the sofa, surrounded by boxes. "I'm exhausted," Tess began. "Thank goodness I have the weekend off before I start work on Monday. Do you think we'll be able to finish unpacking by then?"

"Of course we will. Once I take the boxes out of the house, it will look much better."

"I'm so glad Mattie likes her room."

Sebastian sipped his wine. "She's just like you—taking it all in stride. I can't believe we're actually here. I never would have guessed we'd end up living in London."

"You say it like you're unsure of our decision," Tess said with concern.

"No, I'm happy to make the move. It was just an unexpected surprise, that's all," he explained. "I can still work for Fiona. I get to see Penny and Sigourney. I was even thinking about finding my father."

"We're here now. There's nothing to stop you. Maybe you can contact Max and Victoria and they'd be willing to tell you what they remember about him," Tess suggested. "Do you think they'd talk to you? How much influence does Lily really have over them?"

Sebastian shrugged. "I haven't talked to them in years. It's not a bad idea. Maybe they can tell me something to give the private investigator a place to start his search—once I hire an investigator. I'll talk to Sigourney later. Right now, I need to make sure we're settled in."

Tess leaned into Sebastian and hugged him. "I have a good feeling about this. I think something amazing is going to happen."

Sebastian kissed the top of her head. "I hope you're right."

# Chapter 4 - The World Where You Live

The flat was unpacked and looking neat and organized. Sebastian and Mattie had sent Tess off to work with a kiss—now all he had to do was entertain a four-year-old. That probably wouldn't be hard, since they were living in the cultural center of England.

Sebastian guided Mattie through the rooms at the Tate Gallery, holding her small, delicate hand in his. Something caught her eye and she pulled her father toward the painting.

She looked up to him and said, "Pick me up, Daddy. I want to see better."

Sebastian obliged, lifting her up and cradling her in his arms. "You're getting too big, Mattie." He smiled, secretly delighted that she still loved to be held by him.

She studied the painting of several women walking down a curved stone staircase, playing musical instruments. They were wearing thin, gossamer tunics and their red spirals of hair were elegantly coiffed atop their heads. "I like this one. It's pretty. Who made it?"

"This painting is by Sir Edward Burne-Jones. It was painted in 1880."

"Wow, that's old."

"Yes, it is," Sebastian agreed. "What do you like about the painting?" he quizzed his daughter.

"They look like angels, Daddy."

"Do you notice how they all have the same face?"

Mattie nodded. "Why is that, Daddy?"

"Well, you see, the woman who posed for the painter was his muse."

"What's a muse?" the child asked.

"A muse is someone who inspires you to create beautiful things," Sebastian explained. "The painter was so inspired by this woman, he made all the ladies in the painting look just like her."

"Was he married to her?"

Sebastian chuckled. How on earth did this little one come up with these questions? "No, he wasn't married to her." He didn't have the heart to tell her the muse was the artist's mistress—nor did he want to explain to his four-year-old what a mistress was.

"Was he in love with her?" Mattie countered.

"Yes, he was madly in love with her," Sebastian replied, touching the tip of his nose to hers. "Just like I'm madly in love with you."

"I love you, too," Mattie replied with a giggle.

He gently set her back down on her feet and looked at his Rolex. "It's almost noon. We should get going if we're going to meet your mum for lunch."

"We can come back here later?"

"Absolutely," her father agreed.


They made their way down the marble staircase and toward the main entrance door. "Daddy, my shoe is untied," Mattie said, looking down at her long shoelace that was resting on the floor.

"Do you want me to tie it for you?" Sebastian offered to help.

"No, I can do it." She bent over and meticulously made two loops with the shoe strings and tied them. Sebastian watched intently until she finished the task. She stood up and took her father's hand and almost bumped into an older woman as she took a step forward.

Sebastian stopped in his tracks. The woman standing in front of him was his mother. She hadn't changed at all. She still wore a tailored designer suit, sensible pumps, and her hair was pulled back in the usual updo. His mouth went dry. It had been seven years since their disastrous encounter—the encounter that changed his life for the better.

"Sebastian?" She said his name in the form of a question, obviously taken aback to find him standing in front of her after all these years. She turned to observe the small, adorable child standing next to him, who had Sebastian's brown hair and blue eyes.

Sebastian said nothing. Mattie finally broke the silence. "Hello," she cheerfully greeted.

"Hello, I'm Lady Lily Irons," Lily responded. "And who might you be?"

"I'm Mattie Irons. We have the same last name!" Mattie extended her small hand to shake her grandmother's.

Sebastian instinctively stood in front of Mattie to act as a buffer between his mother and his daughter. Mattie peered around his thigh.

"This is your child?" Lily asked in amazement.

Sebastian turned and protectively picked Mattie up in his arms. "Come on, Mattie. We'll be late for lunch with your mum."

"Do we get to take the Tube?" Mattie asked with enthusiasm.

"Yes, we'll go on a little adventure," Sebastian smiled.

Mattie turned back to face Lily. "It was nice to meet you," she said as Sebastian quickly brushed past his mother and eagerly exited the museum.

Once outside, the cool air hit Sebastian in the face and snapped him out of his shock. He continued to hold Mattie in his arms, and with a quick pace walked down the road toward Pimlico Station. A heavy sigh escaped his lips.

"Daddy, was that lady our family?" she asked, looking back over her father's shoulder.

"No, Mattie," he curtly replied.

"But she has the same last name as we do," she protested.

"Yes. But you'll find that just because someone shares your last name, that does not make them family."

"Aunt Sigourney is family."

"And so is Aunt Alice, Uncle Henry, and Aunt Penny, but they don't have our last name," Sebastian politely reminded her. What was he doing trying to reason with a four year old? He decided to change the subject. "How about we pick up some flowers for mummy in the train station? What should we buy her?"

Thankfully, Mattie was easily distracted. "A big bouquet! We should get Gerbera daisies and roses and tiger lilies."

"Tiger lilies? I don't think they're in season right now."

"I don't care, Daddy. I like the name. Grrrr!" She scrunched her nose, bared her teeth, and clawed her hands up in his face to mimic a tiger cub.

"Oh, you're a very scary tiger, indeed."


Sebastian and Mattie entered the Associated Press building and rode the elevator to the twenty-fifth floor. They walked over to the front desk and Sebastian introduced himself. "Hello, we're here to see Tess Irons. Can you please let her know her husband and daughter are here to take her to lunch?"

The receptionist smiled down at Mattie and then picked up the receiver to make the call. A few minutes later, Tess was walking toward them.

"We bought you flowers for your first day of work," a beaming Mattie announced.

Tess looked at the large bouquet of daisies and roses. "I love them, thank you. Let's go put them on my desk and I'll grab my purse and we can be on our way."

Tess walked them through a maze of cubicles. There was a busy excitement in the newsroom: people on the phone, some typing away on computers, others rushing about the floor. It was controlled chaos and Sebastian understood immediately why Tess loved her job. They entered the three-walled cubicle and Mattie took a seat in her mother's swivel chair. Tess placed the vase of flowers next to the photo of the three of them in Central Park.

"Come, Mattie. Mummy only has an hour for lunch," Sebastian reminded his daughter.

They sat in a nearby park, eating take-away sandwiches while Mattie ran around the lush green grass, burning off energy. "How is your first day going?" Sebastian asked, after swallowing a bite of his prawn sandwich.

"Good, I thought it might be hard, but the procedures are the same, it's just getting to know everyone on the team. I'm happy." Tess sat back and gave Sebastian a long, hard look. "How is your day? You seem a little off. Is Mattie driving you crazy?"

"I took Mattie to the Tate Gallery this morning and had the misfortune to run into Lily."

"Oh my God, what happened?"

"We bumped into her as we were leaving. Mattie was all talk and smiles. I was in shock—all I could think about was getting Mattie out of there and protecting her."

"You did, Bas. You're an amazing father," Tess said to comfort him.

"Lily was gobsmacked to see me with a child in tow."

"Yes, I would imagine so." Tess reached over and took his hand. "She doesn't know where we live. She cut you out of the family. Please don't let this rattle you."

"I suppose you're right. It wouldn't be realistic to think I could live in London and not run into her eventually." Sebastian let out a weary sigh. "I guess it is better that it happened sooner than later."

"Sebastian, you take care of us, you protect us. There is no one else I'd ever want to have my back. I love you."

He pulled Tess into his arms and hugged her tight. "Thank you, darling," he whispered in her ear. "You're right. She can't hurt us. I won't let her."

Tess looked at her wrist watch. "I've got to be getting back. We can talk more tonight, I promise."

Sebastian picked up the rubbish and placed it in the brown paper bag. "Mattie, come on. It's time to go," he called out to this daughter.

# Chapter 5 - Into My Life

Sebastian and Mattie walked Tess back to work, giving her hugs and kisses before they headed for the Tube. "Daddy, can we stop in and see Aunt Penny?"

"Mattie, you saw her a few days ago," Sebastian reasoned.

"But I want to hear about the ball!" she protested.

Sebastian checked the time. "Well, I reckon we can pop in and see if she's home."

"Yay!" Mattie exclaimed, jumping up and down.

They rode to Kensington High Street Station and walked to Penny's townhouse. Mattie rushed up the front steps and was knocking on the red door before Sebastian had a chance to ring the doorbell.

Penny opened the door, wearing a navy dress and heels, her long blonde hair gently falling over her shoulders. She looked as if she were ready to go on a date. "Well, hello. This is an unexpected visit," Penny greeted.

Sebastian leaned in and kissed her cheek. "Sorry to pop in unannounced, but someone was eager to hear about the ball."

Penny crouched down to Mattie's level and gave her a hug. "Come in—I was just about to have tea."

The trio walked into the parlor. A tall man in a bespoke gray suit stood by the window, his attention focused on something outside. Sebastian recognized him immediately. The man turned to face them with a smile.

"Maxwell," Sebastian said, shocked to see his brother standing in front of him.

"Sebastian, it's been too long. It is good to see you again," Max said, extending his hand.

They shook hands and Sebastian looked at Penny, hoping to get a glimpse of what was going on, but he couldn't read her expression.

"And who do we have here?" Max inquired, looking down at Mattie.

"I'm Mattie Irons," she announced, holding out her small hand to Max.

"Hello, Mattie. I'm your Uncle Max."

"Are you Aunt Penny's boyfriend?" the brazen four-year-old asked without shame.

"Martha, that's not a polite question to ask someone you've just met," Sebastian chided.

Thankfully, Penny jumped into the conversation. "Mattie, will you help me get the tea from the kitchen and bring it in here so we can enjoy some refreshments?"

The girls left the room, leaving Sebastian and Maxwell alone. Sebastian hadn't seen Max in six or seven years. He couldn't actually recall how long it had been. "I'm sorry, I'm surprised to see you here." Sebastian walked over the sideboard and poured himself a finger of scotch. He motioned to Max, who declined the drink.

"I ran into Penny at the ball the other evening. She invited me to stop by for tea," Max explained. "I'm sorry about everything that transpired between you and mother. I just wanted you to know that it doesn't matter to me. I'm still your brother."

Sebastian let out the breath he'd been holding in. "Thank you, Max. That means a lot to me."

"Sigourney kept me abreast of what's been happening in your life. A wife and a child—who would have thunk?"

Sebastian chuckled. "Life can be unexpected at times."

"You look very happy. I'm glad things worked out for you."

Penny and Mattie walked back into the room pushing a tea trolley. "Okay, you two sit down. Tea is served," Penny said.

The four of them sat around the coffee table, sipping tea and eating finger sandwiches. *Life could certainly be unexpected*, Sebastian thought to himself as Penny and Max regaled Mattie with stories from the charity ball they had attended.

"So I'm standing at the podium ready to make my speech, when I reach into my suit pocket to realize I've forgotten my papers I had the speech written on!" Max exclaimed.

"He had this look of sheer panic on his face," Penny added.

"I was in a panic. I've been juggling so many charities, I couldn't remember the name of those I was supposed to thank."

"Luckily, I noticed the speech lying on the floor under his chair."

"It must have fallen out of my pocket."

"So I decide to walk up to the podium and hand it to him. Just as I hit the top stair, my heel got caught in the hem of my dress and…"

"Penny starts to fall, face first and…"

"Maxwell rushes over and catches me before I hit the ground. Utterly embarrassing!"

Mattie sat wide-eyed witnessing the verbal banter. There was definitely more going on than met the eye, and Sebastian couldn't wait to get Penny alone to find out what that might be.

An hour later, the clock on the mantle chimed. "Mattie, we should be going. I'm sure Aunt Penny and Uncle Max have things to discuss."

Max stood. "Sebastian, here's my card. Ring me. I'd like to have lunch with you soon," he said, pulling it from the inside pocket of his suit.

Sebastian accepted the card. "I'd like that, Maxwell. It was good to see you again." Next he kissed Penny on the cheek and whispered in her ear, "We'll talk about this later."

Penny merely grinned as she walked Sebastian and Mattie to the front door.

Tess made it home around six o'clock. They sat at the dinner table and Mattie proceeded to tell Tess about her meeting with Uncle Max. Tess listened with great interest while she stole glances at Sebastian to gauge his reaction.

They put Mattie to bed at eight o'clock and finally they were alone. "Lily and your brother on the same day, the first week we move to London. Are you okay?" Tess asked with concern.

"Max was nice. He invited me to lunch so we can talk. He seemed genuinely happy for us."

"That would be the perfect opportunity to ask him about your father."

"Exactly. Only now that I have the chance to get some answers, I'm nervous," he admitted.

"It's only natural," Tess reasoned. "You're going to try to find a man that doesn't even know you exist."

"The first step is to assemble information. There's no saying I have to meet him if he's found."

"That's true, but isn't the whole point of the exercise to find him, meet him, see if you can have a relationship?" Tess asked.

Sebastian held up his hand as if to stop her. "One step at a time, please." He leaned his head back on the couch and looked up at the ceiling. "I'm more curious to know what Max was doing in Penny's home. I know you joked about them dating, but I can't help but feel there was some sexual tension there."

"I know—you can ask Max and I'll corner Penny. Maybe we can play matchmaker after all," Tess said, excited by the prospect.

"Brilliant, now you and Mattie are ganging up on me," he smirked.

"Countess Penelope has a nice ring to it."

"Technically, you would address her as Lady Penelope, the Countess of Sutton."

"Why do you English have to make things so complicated?"

"Would you prefer we say 'hey you' in a New York accent?"

Tess laughed. "Could you imagine Lily's expression if you did that?"

Sebastian had to laugh, too. "Let's not put the cart before the horse. Penny's on several charity boards, and I imagine Max is too, now that he's retired from Irons Electronic to become the Earl of Sutton."

"Do you think he's living in the castle?"

"I would think so—most likely in the fall and winter. He's probably spending the spring and summer in London due to all the events he needs to attend during the social season."

"You've sort of lost me," Tess admitted.

"You should have watched more *Masterpiece Theatre,*" Sebastian joked.

"Why should I watch TV to learn about the English upper crust when I have you to explain it to me?"

Sebastian pulled her into his arms. "Enough talk of titles, balls, and betrothals. I just want to enjoy some quiet time with my wife. What do you say we turn in early?"

"I can't sleep thinking about all these possibilities. Who knew moving here would be so exciting? Sometimes I wonder if I shouldn't be writing for the social pages instead of world news."

Sebastian stood from the couch. "I didn't say anything about sleeping," he said in a deep, sexy voice.

"In that case, let's go," Tess agreed, pulling him by the hand toward their bedroom.

Once they were inside their bedroom, Sebastian locked the door and then leaned against it, watching his wife as she slowly undressed, making a show of it for him. Although she was no-nonsense Hamilton at work, she'd definitely learned to let loose in the bedroom.

Tess sauntered toward her husband and pinned him up against the door, leaning in and covering his mouth with hers. He swore he would never tire of her passionate kisses as long as he lived. He slipped off his navy suit coat as Tess untied his silk striped tie. Next she began to unbutton his shirt while he removed his belt and unzipped his trousers.

Tess began to kiss the hard plane of his chest and then licked her way down to his erect cock. Taking it in her hand, she stroked up and down, flicking her tongue over the shiny head. Sebastian leaned against the door and splayed his hands along the wall. "Just like that, darling," he hissed out between shallow breaths. After a few more strokes, she stood up and kissed him again.

Sebastian let his hands roam down the soft smooth skin of her back and then he cupped her buttocks. Turning her around, he pushed her against the door and lifted her off the ground. Tess' legs instinctively wrapped around his waist as he slipped inside her. Careful not to hit her head against the door, he thrust in and out at a languid pace.

"Do you want to finish this here or on the bed?" Tess asked in between kisses. Sebastian backed away from the door and carried Tess to their bed. He lay back, leaving her on top of him. She smiled as her hand ran over his shoulders and down his biceps. "I'll never get tired of making love with you," Tess whispered as she rocked back and forth astride his body.

"Good, because you're mine—forever," he said, taking hold of her hips and pushing deeper inside her. The quick movement made Tess climax and she collapsed onto Sebastian's chest, her long brown hair tickling his neck. He smoothed her hair over with his right hand while his left hand traced the curve of her spine.

Tess lifted her head and looked at her husband. "I'm yours, but we're not finished yet," she purred as she rolled off his chest and took his erection in her hand.

Sebastian closed his eyes and concentrated on his wife's touch. Her hands were soft and warm, her mouth was heaven. He took his hand and guided her head closer to his body—needing to feel her mouth surrounding every inch of him. Sebastian was so close to the edge, one more stroke and he came undone. "Fuck," he moaned as he tangled his fingers in Tess' hair. She crept up his body, giving him a sweet kiss on the neck before laying her head on his shoulder.

# Chapter 6 - It's Only Natural

The events of the past week had finally tired Mattie out, and Sebastian was given a few blessed hours of silence while she napped. He couldn't stop thinking about his impromptu meeting with Maxwell the day before. It could have been completely harmless, a situation of circumstance, but something nagged at Sebastian's consciousness, telling him there was more than met the eye.

He picked up the receiver and phoned Penny.

"Hello," she said on the other end of the line.

"Hello, Penny."

"I wondered how long it would take for you to ring me."

"What's going on with you and Maxwell?"

"I don't know that it's any of your business," she stated, her tone light and airy.

"Well, when you say it like that, I know there is more going on than meets the eye."

"Sebastian, we travel in the same circles. I asked him to tea. Why does this trouble you?"

Sebastian sighed. He didn't actually have an answer to her question. "I don't know, Pen."

"Are you jealous because another man is showing me some attention?" she teased.

Maybe she had a point. Maybe he was a little jealous. "He's not good enough for you," he replied, frowning.

"Sebastian, you hardly know him! Just because he's your mother's son doesn't make him a bad person," Penny scolded.

He didn't want to argue with her; he simply wanted to be sure that she was treated properly. His brother was the Earl of Sutton, for Christ's sake—of course Maxwell was a gentleman. "I'm sorry, Pen. I don't know Max very well. I'm being absurd."

"Finally, you've got some common sense," she admitted. "There's nothing romantic going on between Max and I, but I do enjoy his company. He's a good person. I suggest you take him up on the offer for lunch and get to know your brother a little better. I know the age gap you share prevented you for forming a close relationship, but you're adults. There's no reason you can't start being friends now."

"You're right. He's not Lily. I do want to get to know him better."

"Then it's settled. Ring him and meet him for lunch. You can even leave Mattie with me so you two can really talk. I'm sure there's much to sort out."

"You have no idea," Sebastian muttered.

"What do you mean by that?" Penelope asked with great curiosity.

"Nothing, just thinking aloud. Thank you, Penny." He set the receiver down and pondered his next move.

Mattie walked out of her bedroom, rubbing the sleep from her eyes. She walked over to Sebastian and curled up on the couch with him. "What are you doing, Daddy?"

"I'm reading Mummy's article in the newspaper."

"Is it good?" she asked, leaning her head against his arm.

"Yes, it's very good."

"Can we go to the park this afternoon?"

"I have a better idea. Why don't we go visit Aunt Sigourney?" Sebastian asked, looking down at this daughter.

"Yay! Let's go!"

They traveled by Tube to Marble Arch station, then walked to Sigourney's flat in Mayfair. Sebastian lifted Mattie into his arms so she could ring the doorbell.

Sigourney opened the door with a wide smile gracing her face. "Hello! Come inside."

Mattie kissed her on the cheek first, followed by Sebastian. An adorable English toy spaniel came running into the foyer, his shiny amber coat blowing in the breeze. Mattie squirmed in Sebastian's arms. "Let me down, Daddy!"

Sebastian laughed. "What have we here?" he said, crouching down to pet the dog.

"This is Monty," Sigourney introduced.

"Is it a girl or a boy dog?" Mattie asked.

"It's a boy and he's six months old."

"Daddy, I want a dog," Mattie said, looking at her father.

"Maybe later."

"Come out to the garden. We'll have some tea and Mattie and Monty can run off their excess energy."

Sebastian and Sigourney sat outside at the café table, watching the child and puppy play fetch with a red rubber ball.

"She's grown so much, Sebastian. It's good to see you again. I'm so glad you and Tess decided to make the move to London."

"It's been an eventful first week, I'll tell you."

Sigourney raised her eyebrow at him, but didn't say a word.

"Mattie and I ran into Lily at the Tate Gallery."

"So I heard. You really threw her for loop. She had no idea you had a child," Sigourney informed him. "Of course that led to me getting the third degree."

"What did you tell her?"

"I just confirmed you have a bright, gregarious four-year-old. And I may have also told her you're deliriously happy being a husband and father," Sigourney said with a wink.

Sebastian reached over and squeezed his sister's hand in gratitude. "Thank you."

"It's the truth. I understand why you had to break ranks with Mummy. I think you're a better man for it. If she can't get past it, that's her fault."

"I'm really here to talk about Maxwell. I bumped into him at Penny's the other day. They were having tea. Do you know anything about this?" he asked in a guarded tone.

"You know it is Max's first season as Earl. They seem to have struck up a friendship. Penny's sort of showing him the ropes, helping with the various charity committees."

"So you don't think there is anything romantic going on, then?"

Sigourney laughed. "You're not her father, Sebastian! Why are you so concerned?"

"She's a dear friend. I don't want to see her hurt."

"He's our brother."

"And I hardly know him."

"Then do something about that. He's a good man—if you give him a chance."

He eyed her with suspicion. "So Lily doesn't dictate what he does?"

"No, Maxwell is very much his own person." Sigourney glanced over to see Monty licking Mattie's face and chuckled. "Penelope Stanton could do a lot worse than Max." Sigourney sipped her tea. "Enough about our brother. Tell me about Tess. Does she love it here? How is her new job?"

"She's very happy. Tess has finally gotten everything she longed for when she graduated. I'm surprised it happened so quickly, but as long as my girls are happy, I'm happy."

Mattie rushed over to the table. "Do you have any treats for Monty?"

Sigourney handed her a small dog biscuit off the table. "Here you go. You must instruct him to sit before you give it to him, however." Mattie ran off.

"How is the orchestra?" Sebastian asked.

"I'm really enjoying it. You and Tess should come to a performance soon."

"I'd like that very much."

As soon as Tess walked through the front door, Mattie came tearing into the room and jumped into her arms. "Mummy, guess what? Daddy said we could get a puppy if you're okay with it. Can we?" The child looked at Tess with so much hope and desire, Tess was at a loss for words. She looked to Sebastian for help.

"Martha, I told you your mum and I will discuss it. I didn't agree to getting a puppy, so don't try being charming to get your way," Sebastian warned.

Tess laughed. "She comes by it naturally," she said, leaning in to kiss Sebastian on the lips. She set Mattie down on the floor. "Now why do you want a puppy?"

"Aunt Sigourney has one. His name is Monty."

"Daddy and I will talk about it when you go to bed tonight."

"Okay, I'm ready now. I'll get my PJs on," she announced.

"Mattie, we have to have dinner first. Don't be so impatient," Sebastian chided.

The little girl pouted and then walked over to the dinner table and took a seat.

"This should be fun," Tess muttered, taking her husband's hand and walking toward the table.

"You sit while I get dinner."

They ate their meal while Mattie talked nonstop about getting a puppy and how much she would love it. When a break in the conversation finally took place, Tess asked Sebastian, "Did you decide to go see Max?"

Sebastian nodded his head. "I phoned him this afternoon. We're having lunch tomorrow at The Ivy. Penny offered to watch Mattie."

Tess observed him closely, unsure if he was happy or nervous about the impending meeting. "It will be fine. Just think what you could learn. This could be a big step for you—the start of the investigation."

"I hope you're right, Tess."

# Chapter 7 - Brothers in Arms

Sebastian waited outside The Ivy for Maxwell. His brother pulled up in a chauffeured car. Sebastian laughed. He had done the same thing years ago, the last time he had eaten there with Penny. Today he took the Tube.

Max greeted Sebastian with a handshake and then the two brothers walked inside the restaurant, where they were promptly seated for lunch. The place hadn't change since the last time he'd visited. Sebastian loved the dark wood paneling and stained glass windows. It was still one of his favorite restaurants in London.

Maxwell selected an aged French fine wine from the sommelier. Once they were alone, Max sat back in his chair and eyed Sebastian. "I'm glad you agreed to meet me."

"We don't really know each other, do we? As long as Lily doesn't threaten to disown you, I suppose there is no harm."

"There's always two sides to every story, Sebastian. I'd like to get yours."

"It was a long time ago, Max. Why rehash it? If you truly want to have a relationship, I'd like that. You'll find I'm a better, much happier person when we can leave Lily out of the mix," he admitted, taking a sip of his water.

"Mother can't harm me. I outrank her," Max said lightly, making a joke.

His easy attitude made Sebastian laugh aloud: he wasn't expecting it. Maybe Penny and Sigourney were right in their advice after all. "Yes, how do you enjoy being an earl? Is it better than working for Irons Electronics?"

"It's certainly different, I'll grant you that. Thank goodness I don't have to serve in the House of Commons—although sometimes those charity committees are just as bad."

"Penelope Stanton has been helping out though. That must be some relief."

"Tell me more about Penelope," Max said as the sommelier came back to the table with the wine.

After the ritual of uncorking, sniffing the cork, and tasting the wine, Max nodded his acceptance to the waiter.

"Ah, so that's why you really asked me to luncheon," Sebastian realized.

"You two are friends, aren't you?" Max asked in confusion.

"Yes, we are *very* good friends. Do you have romantic notions for her?" Sebastian asked straight out.

"It's early days, yet. I do find myself thinking about her at the oddest times, though."

"Thinking what?"

"She's beautiful, smart, graceful…"

Sebastian cut him off. "In other words, she'd be the perfect wife for an earl?"

"Yes." Max sipped his wine. "You can't blame me for thinking it. I'm bound by duty to marry and raise a family. The earldom should be kept in the Irons family."

Sebastian gave him a leery look. "And Lily has nothing to do with this?"

"For God's sakes, Sebastian, stop being so paranoid. I'm thirty-five years old and want to settle down. Mother has nothing to do with it. I want your opinion of Penelope. Do you think she likes me? Should I pursue her?"

Sebastian glared at Max. "She's not wild animal to be hunted down," he clipped out.

"Were you two involved? I always thought she was with Prince Alistair all those years ago."

"Maxwell, I'm not going to sit here in public and discuss my sex life," Sebastian whispered, annoyed.

Max hung his head in frustration. "I admit, I'm handling this all wrong." He took a deep breath and started again. "Tell me what you've been doing since you've moved to America. Every time I see Sigourney, she always sings your praises."

"In a nutshell: I found my soul mate, got married, had a beautiful child, and support my family by working in an art gallery."

"That's all I want, too. I want to find my soul mate."

"That's a very un-earl-like thing to say. Matches should be dictated by class and reputation," Sebastian stated.

"It's the twentieth century. I want a wife I love. I don't want to end up like mother and father, hating each other."

Aha: there was Sebastian's chance to bringing up his father, so he jumped at the opportunity. "What do you remember about our father?"

Maxwell squirmed uncomfortably in his chair.

"There must be something you can tell me. I know his name is Martin Baker."

"How did you know that?" Max asked, surprised by the admission.

"When Nanny died, she left me a letter and a photo. I've been thinking about finding him. I could really use your help. What can you tell me about him?"

Maxwell was silent for some time. Finally he said, "I remember him being far less strict than Mother. He would always play with me and Victoria when he was around. But the older we grew, the more he was away—having one of his many affairs, I suppose."

"You've never had contact with him over the years?"

"No. I have a feeling Mother was paying him to stay away. If he tried to contact us, he'd be cut off."

Sebastian snickered. "What kind of man would give up his children for money?"

"Precisely."

"Lily accused me of being just like him," Sebastian confessed.

"I've seen you with your daughter. I don't believe you're anything like him at all."

Sebastian smiled, thankful for the compliment. "I just want to know what happened to him. Nanny said he doesn't even know I exist. What if he has changed?"

Maxwell nodded his head in agreement. "Yes, anything is possible. If you choose to pursue this, I'll help you in any way I can."

"Don't you ever wonder what's happened to him?" Sebastian wanted to know.

"Not really. I just assumed he had no interest in seeing me. After all, he does know who I am and where I live. For you, it's a different situation all together. I understand your need to meet him. Just prepare yourself: it may not have a happy ending."

The waiter appeared to take their order. Max ordered fillet—rare—while Sebastian opted for the salmon. The waiter bowed and left them to their conversation.

"What do you remember about the day he left?" Sebastian asked next.

"Mother had the three of us file into the nursery. She sat us down and explained that she and Father were getting a divorce and we were never to speak of him again. Then she proceeded to tell us we would go by the family name of Irons from that day forward."

"That must have been an odd meeting for a child."

Maxwell shrugged his shoulders. "It was Mother, so it really was nothing out of the ordinary. Honestly, she was so angry, Victoria and I didn't need her taking her wrath out on us, so we just kept quiet. Thankfully, Sigourney was too young to understand."

Sebastian knew all too well what it was like to be on the receiving end of Lily's anger. Max and Victoria were only kids—what could they have done? "I was initially thinking of hiring an investigator so see if he could find Martin. If he was found, then I would decide if I wanted to meet him or not."

"I have some contacts. Why don't you bring your family out to the castle for the weekend? We'll put our heads together and see what we can come up with."

Sebastian shuddered at the thought. When he left the castle after Lily had disowned him, he naturally assumed it would be the last time he ever set foot on the property. "I can't, Max. Not if there is any chance Lily might show up. I need to protect my family," Sebastian tried to explain.

"I'll make sure she's not there. You have my word. Please, I want to meet this amazing wife of yours and it would be nice to have a little one running about the grounds again." Max paused, then said off the cuff, "I wanted to invite Penelope as well. You can be our chaperone. What do you say?"

The very last thing Sebastian expected was an invitation to spend the weekend in the country with Maxwell. He was a sly one with his ulterior motives. Penny was a grown woman. She could make up her own mind. There was no saying she would even accept the invitation. Sebastian grinned. "All right, you should invite Sigourney and Victoria, too. Might as well make it a party."

"Excellent! Next weekend then?"

"Yes, next weekend."

The waiter arrived with their lunch and the siblings went quiet as they ate their meal.

# Chapter 8 - Sutton Castle Revisited

Friday evening, Sebastian drove Penny and his family out to Sutton on Ashfield. They were taking Penny's Jaguar, since Sebastian didn't own a car. Tess sat in the front passenger seat while Penny and Mattie chatted in the back seat.

They crested the familiar hill and soon the castle was in sight. The great stone monstrosity stood amid the verdant, well-kept grounds. "Are you going to be okay with this?" Tess asked with concern.

"I never thought I see this place again," he admitted. "It feels odd to be back."

"Daddy, is that your house?" Mattie asked leaning forward between her parents.

"No, it's Uncle Max's house, but I used to live here a long time ago."

"It looks like Cinderella's castle."

Sebastian chuckled at his beautiful, naïve daughter. Living there was never a fairy tale—it was more like a nightmare. But there were some good times with Nanny and this was her final resting place, so Sebastian still had a connection to the castle. Now that it belonged to Max, things might be different— better. Sebastian was in a good place now; maybe it was time to move forward with his brother and sister. If he could have a positive relationship with all his siblings, he was willing to put in the effort.

They pulled up in front of the entrance and parked the car. A brigade of servants filed out the door to assist with the luggage. The last person out the door was Maxwell. "Welcome home," he said with a genuine smile.

Tess wrapped her arm around Sebastian's and returned the smile. "Maxwell, it's nice to meet you."

Max leaned in and kissed her cheek. "Sebastian has told me so much about you. I'm glad you could make it out this weekend."

Mattie marched right up to Max and extended her hand, "Hi, Uncle Max."

Maxwell picked her up and gave her a hug. "Hello, Mattie." He went on to shake his brother's hand and kiss Penny on both cheeks. "Everyone, get settled in.

Dinner will be at eight o'clock. Someone will show you to your rooms."

The group trooped into the marble foyer with its tall ceiling and grand staircase. Penny looked at Sebastian and grinned. "The last time I was here, I was kissing you goodbye."

"The last time I was here, we were scattering Nanny Jones' ashes," Tess added.

"The last time I was here, I was disinherited," Sebastian commented as if it were a competition to see who could come up with the best story.

"What does that mean?" Mattie asked as Sebastian lifted her in his arms to walk up the staircase to their rooms.

"I'll tell you some other time, okay, darling?"

Max had the nursery made up for Mattie. It didn't look any different from when Sebastian had resided there, but everything was bright, airy, and freshly cleaned. Tess unpacked her daughter's suitcase and then put her in pajamas. Sebastian tucked her into bed. He picked a book from the bookcase and read a little bit of *The Tales of Peter Rabbit* by Beatrix Potter. Soon she had dozed off and he and Tess quietly left the room.

Their guest room was a few doors down the hall. The servants had laid out their luggage along with a tea service and fresh cut roses from the garden. "I was wondering if they would put us in your old room," Tess said as she looked around, surveying the king-sized canopy bed.

"I wouldn't be surprised if Lily took every stick of furniture and burnt it after she kicked us out," he lightheartedly responded. "Let's freshen up for dinner. There will be cocktails beforehand."

They showered and changed. Sebastian wore a navy suit, white shirt, and gray striped tie. Tess dressed in her black Chanel. They walked down to the sitting room hand in hand. Entering through the open double doors, they found Maxwell, Sigourney, Penny, and Victoria were all seated, drinking cocktails.

Victoria stood when they entered the room. She was statuesque, with long brown hair and high cheek bones. She was more of a classic beauty compared to Sigourney's supermodel looks. "Sebastian, it is good to see you again." She hugged her brother and then greeted Tess.

Sebastian was a little taken aback by her welcoming manner. He had always assumed his older twin siblings were on Lily's side. How strange that they were welcoming him back home with open arms. He prayed it wasn't some sort of terrible hoax and that he wasn't the butt of the joke. He shook his head to clear out the negative thoughts. "I'm sorry, it's just odd to be back here. It's been so long since we've spoken. I'm not sure Lily would approve of you and Maxwell being so nice to me."

"Sebastian, she has nothing to do with this. You are back in England. I want to get reacquainted with you and your family. I'm truly happy to see you again."

Sebastian nodded his thanks and headed for the drink trolley. He poured himself a scotch and then pulled the bottle of champagne from the ice bucket and poured a glass for Tess. They had only been there for a few minutes when the butler appeared in the entryway and announced "Dinner is served."

The group gathered in the formal dining room. Maxwell and Sebastian sat at the table ends, while the ladies sat on the sides. As the meal began, Sebastian observed Max and Penny across the table. Occasionally, Penny would reach over and touch Maxwell's arm. They would smile at one another, lean in to whisper a discreet comment, and laugh. Sebastian only wished he could hear them better, but their voices were drowned out by Victoria and Tess' conversation.

"Tell me Tess, how did you and Sebastian fall in love?" Victoria asked.

Tess pondered her question and then began. "It's a long, complicated story. I'm not really sure where to begin."

"But it has a happy ending—that is evident."

Tess looked over at her husband and smiled. "Yes, a very happy ending." She took sip of champagne and asked, "Will you be running Irons Electronics when Lily decides to retire?"

"If she ever decides to retire. Yes, I get my happy ending too."

"You're not married?"

"No, I don't have time for it. The company keeps me busy and that makes me happy. Maxwell is the heir, Sigourney the creative one, Sebastian is the black sheep, and I'm the dutiful daughter."

Sigourney turned to Sebastian. "I told you it would be okay to come here for the weekend."

"The weekend has just begun. Anything can happen."

"Why do you worry so? You have everything you've ever wanted from life."

"Exactly," Sebastian agreed. "That's why I don't want to tempt fate."

"Mummy hasn't kicked me out of the family and I've flat-out told her I will continue to fraternize with you whether she likes it or not. What if she walked into this room right now? What if the three of us stood up to her and said, 'we don't care if you disinherited Sebastian, he is our brother and we won't betray him?'"

"I'd prefer not to test that scenario. Can't we just enjoy this delightful meal—in peace?"

Sigourney chuckled. "What's a little drama?"

"I've had enough drama to last me two lifetimes. I'm through with it. Please, can't we just have a nice weekend where no one pops up out of the blue or gets into an argument or dies?"

"Well, now that's a tall order to fill," Sigourney mumbled under her breath.

After dinner, the ladies went back to the sitting room to talk about whatever it is ladies talk about, while Maxwell and Sebastian retired to the smoking room. The room was small, with a massive fireplace that overtook the space. The walls were painted maroon, and dark Dutch paintings hung on the walls. Max sat down on the old leather chair and pulled a cigar from his suit coat pocket. He offered one to Sebastian, who held up his hand to decline.

"I haven't smoked in years. Tess never liked it and I have a child in the house now. I'll just enjoy my scotch." He took the seat opposite Maxwell.

"I've been in contact with a private investigator—someone discreet. I've set up a meeting for Tuesday afternoon in my office in London. Can you make it?"

"So soon?" Sebastian asked, surprised by Maxwell's efficient manner.

"It only took a few phone calls," Max said, as if it were no bother at all.

Sebastian chuckled to himself. "Yes, I keep forgetting you're the Earl of Sutton."

"Don't make light of this, Sebastian. Do you or do you not want to find our father?"

Sebastian became somber. "Yes, I want to find him. I just keep thinking, what if it all turns out horribly? Maybe I should leave it be."

Max blew a ring of smoke into the air, pondering the question. "You're not the only person who has wondered. Victoria and I talk about him from time to time."

"Then why not take action? Why wait for me to bring it up?"

Max sipped his brandy and then placed the glass back down on the table. "Maybe you're not the only one afraid of Mother."

"I'm not afraid, Max—not of her." He finished his scotch and placed the empty glass on the arm of the leather chair. "I'll meet you on Tuesday. Now if you don't mind, I'd like to get back to my wife."

Maxwell nodded in agreement as he stood from the chair. "Yes, the ladies await."

Sebastian joined Tess and the others in the sitting room. "Why do you look so serious?" Tess asked.

Sebastian let out the breath he'd been holding in as he placed his arm around Tess' shoulders. "Max set up a meeting with the investigator for Tuesday. I'm shocked that it's happening so quickly. I just need it to sink in."

"It will be okay," Tess reassured. She changed the subject. "I like Victoria. She's ambitious like me."

"Yes, she's the go-getter. I'm glad you like her."

"I think it's good we came back here. It feels like a new beginning."

Sebastian looked about the room—his siblings and Penny laughing and smiling. Everything seemed perfect, but he couldn't shake the odd feeling in his gut that something bad was bound to happen. "Come on, let's go join the others."

# Chapter 9 - In My Life

Sebastian rolled over in bed and looked at the clock on the bedside table. It read 1:30 a.m. and he was wide awake. Quietly, he got out of bed and slipped on his navy robe. He padded down the hallway to the nursery. Inside, Mattie was fast asleep. A four-year-old could only take so much excitement. He sat in the antique rocking chair and watched her sleep peacefully. Whenever anything troubled him, he always found solace in watching his daughter sleep. It was as if everything was put in perspective. Mattie and Tess—they were the reasons he was put on this earth, he was sure of it. So whatever happened next—finding his father, running into Lily, reconnecting with his siblings—he could handle it. Before Sebastian left the nursery, he leaned over and kissed Mattie on the forehead.

He made his way to Nanny's old room. Once inside, he turned on the light. Thankfully, everything was still intact. Lily hadn't removed a thing. This gave him some measure of comfort. He walked around the room looking at old photographs of them together, which made him smile at the long lost memories. "I hope you're proud of me, Nanny," he said aloud as his fingertips touched her image under the glass picture frame. He couldn't help but think how tickled she'd be if she had the chance to know his daughter.

Next he wandered out into the hall and headed for the library. Maybe a nice brandy and a good book would relax him so he could fall asleep. As he turned the corner, he abruptly stopped when he came upon Penny standing outside of Maxwell's bedroom. He stepped back into the shadow as he observed her arms wrapped around Max's neck. She was barefoot, her blonde hair disheveled, as they passionately kissed. When they pulled apart, Penny stepped back and Maxwell closed the door with a soft click.

Penny turned and began to walk toward Sebastian, who took the opportunity to step out in front of her. Startled, Penny jumped and dropped the leather pumps she was holding in her hand. "Dear God Sebastian, must you sneak up on me!" she hissed under her breath.

"I wasn't sneaking up. I was merely taking a walk," he informed her.

"At two in the morning?"

"I couldn't sleep. I see you had the same problem. Only you were undoubtedly having more fun."

"Yes, I was," she smiled.

"Are you happy?"

"Can't you tell?"

"Why didn't you just stay the night with him?"

"We were trying to keep this quiet and avoid a conversation like the one we're having right now. I really like Max. Please be happy for us?"

"If he makes you happy, then I'm happy for you both. I'll keep your secret." He leaned in and kissed her on the cheek. "Goodnight, Pen."

Penny reached out and gently touched his cheek. "You have a beautiful wife and daughter—go back to them. Stop wandering the halls looking so lost. And don't worry about me, I'm a big girl, Sebastian."

He gave her a crooked smile and nodded his head in agreement. "Come, I'll walk you back to your room."

A breakfast buffet was laid out for the guest Saturday morning. The group was going to go on a fox hunt after they finished eating. Sebastian sat next to Tess at the table, eating eggs Benedict and drinking tea. Tess opted for scrambled eggs and toast. Mattie was entertaining Max at the other end of the table. It made Sebastian proud that his daughter was so intelligent and outgoing. She'd inherited those traits from her mother. But her charm—that was all from Sebastian.

"Are you sure you don't mind staying here with Mattie while I hunt? I need to be polite if I want to forge this relationship with Max and Victoria," Sebastian explained as he set the fork on his plate.

"Mattie and I will be fine. I thought I could take her for a walk in the rose garden. She'll love the fountain."

"Maybe this afternoon just the three of us can take the horses out. Mattie has been bugging me to teach her how to ride."

Tess gave him a wary glance. "Are you sure it's safe? She's only four years old, Bas."

"I started riding when I was four. She'll be fine," he reassured his wife.

Maxwell stood from the table. "If everyone is ready, please join me outside."

Mattie joined Tess and Sebastian as the family walked along the marble corridor through the back entrance of the house. Five horses stood, saddled and bridled, at the ready. "I want to go!" Mattie exclaimed, jumping up and down in excitement.

"This afternoon, I promise I'll take you riding. These horses are too big for you. I'll take you out on the pony," Sebastian explained as he knelt down to his daughter's eye level.

She nodded her head in agreement and threw her arms around Sebastian's neck. "Love you, Daddy."

"Love you, too. Now I think Mummy has a surprise for you, so be good and I'll see you at lunch." Sebastian leaned in and kissed Tess on the lips. "I'll be back soon."

The other riders had already mounted their horses, so Sebastian quickly got on the saddle. The foxhounds sprinted off across the verdant grounds and the riders kicked into action in pursuit.

Mattie looked up at Tess and wistfully announced, "I wish we could live here all the time."

"Why is that, Mattie?"

"It's beautiful, and there are lots of pets, and Uncle Max is nice."

"Hmm," was the only thing Tess could come up with in that moment. She watched the riding party crest the last hill, before disappearing from view. "Mattie, I thought you loved our flat in London. Daddy and I have to work in town. We can't live out here. But I bet if you're on your best behavior, Uncle Max will invite us back."

"Awesome!" she said with a big toothy grin.

"Come, I want to show you the rose gardens. There's this really neat fountain with stone fish I want to show you."

Mattie reached up and took Tess' hand, and they walked along the gravel path to the other side of the castle where the garden was located.

Maxwell and Sebastian took a break from the hunt to let their horses drink from a nearby stream. "That daughter of yours is quite delightful, Sebastian. Her vocabulary is astounding for someone her age," Max complimented.

"You better watch out. She'll have you setting up a room for her and visiting on the weekends. She's very taken with you, Max."

"You say that as if you're surprised."

"I'm grateful to reconnect with you and Victoria, but I'm concerned about Lily. I will protect my girls to my last breath. I do not trust Lily. I do not want her anywhere near my family, do you understand?"

"So I reckon suggesting a reconciliation with mother is out of the question?"

"Being disowned was the best thing that ever happened to me. I'm a better man with a happy family. I want to keep it that way. Lily was the one who decided I was no longer welcome in the family. I won't beg her forgiveness." He let out a long, hot breath. "Let's not talk about something so unpleasant on such a lovely day."

"All right," Max agreed as they began to trot the horses up the embankment.

"So how did you sleep last night?" Sebastian asked out of the blue.

"Very well. Shouldn't I be asking you that question? You are a guest in my home, after all."

"I wasn't shagging Penny Stanton last night."

"How did you know?" Maxwell asked, looking like a child caught with his hand in the biscuit jar.

"I couldn't sleep. I saw her coming out of your room. If you wanted to be discreet, why the hell didn't you just let her spend the night in your bed?"

Max was silent.

"She's one of my best friends, Max. She's fancies you. Don't hurt her," Sebastian warned like an overprotective parent.

"I'm quite taken with her as well."

"Then for God's sake, let her spend the entire night in your bed next time—or at least have the decency to make love to her in her own room. You should be the one that leaves in the middle of the night."

"You're right, Sebastian," Maxwell agreed in all seriousness.

Sebastian silently nodded, having reached an unspoken understanding with his brother. Then he kicked the horse into action and took off to join the hunt, Max gaining at a rapid clip.

It had been an exhausting day. Between the lack of sleep the night before, hunting, and teaching Mattie to ride, Sebastian was never more happy to lay his head upon a pillow than he was that evening.

Tess snuggled into his chest.

"Did you have a good day?" he asked Tess as a yawn escaped his lips.

"Yes."

"Thanks for teaching Mattie how to ride. Now I'm afraid she'll start begging for a pony," Tess said with apprehension.

"Maybe she'll give up on asking for a puppy."

Tess chuckled. "I'd rather take care of a dog than a pony."

"Maybe for Christmas," Sebastian agreed.

"You and Maxwell seem to be getting along."

"For now, at least."

"What's that supposed to mean?" Tess inquired, raising her head to look at him.

"I couldn't sleep last night, so I took a walk. I bumped into Penny leaving his room at two in the morning."

Tess grinned. "I knew it! I'm so happy for Penny."

"It's early days, Tess. Don't start planning a wedding yet."

"Ha, that's your job, not mine. I really like Penny, Bas. Wouldn't it be wonderful if she could be as happy as we are?"

Sebastian smiled. He was lucky beyond belief. "It would be wonderful." He closed his eyes and drifted off to sleep.

Sebastian woke with a start as Mattie jumped on top of him. "Daddy, wake up!"

He groaned, reaching for his watch on the nightstand. When his eyes finally focused, he realized it was eight o'clock in the morning. "Mattie, go back to sleep," he muttered to his child.

"But I want to see the pony."

"We have to eat breakfast first, Mattie," Tess chimed in as she sat up in bed.

"I'll go get dressed," her daughter gasped in excitement, jumping off the bed and rushing from the room.

Tess pulled the covers back. "I'll go make sure she coordinates her outfit. Go back to sleep for little while longer." She kissed him on the forehead and then put on her robe before walking toward Mattie's room.

Sebastian and his family joined the others in the breakfast room an hour later. Tess sat next to Penny while Mattie struck up a conversation with Max.

"It looks as if Mattie has made a new best friend this weekend," Penny said, nodding toward her paramour and the little girl at the end of the table.

"Seems to me that Max has made more than one good friend this weekend," Tess smiled.

"Sebastian told you, didn't he?" Penny whispered.

Tess nodded her confirmation. "I'm so happy for you, Penny."

"At least someone in the Irons household is happy for me."

"Don't worry about Sebastian. He'll come around. You know he'll go to any lengths to protect those he loves fiercely. Bas is still a little suspicious of Max. It will take some time for him to realize his loyalty."

Penny nodded. "Yes, I can understand his hesitation after what happened between his mother and him. I think it's a good thing they'll be working together to find his father—it will bring them closer together."

"I hope so," Tess agreed.

# Chapter 10 – Watching the Detectives

Sebastian jogged up the steps of the Westminster Tube Station and turned left to walk down Whitehall Road toward Maxwell's office. A middle-aged personal assistant greeted Sebastian as he opened the door. "Mr. Irons, your brother is waiting for you. Follow me."

Sebastian followed the woman down the short hallway and waited patiently as she knocked on the door. "Enter," a voice said from inside. The assistant opened the door and smiled at Sebastian, who nodded his thanks and stepped inside the office.

It was a simple room furnished with a large cherry desk, a few chairs, and a sofa. It looked as if Max had just moved in and hadn't had time to decorate the space yet. Then Sebastian noticed the tall, thin man in an ill-fitting suit standing behind Maxwell, staring out the window.

"Sebastian, this is Nigel Minton," Max introduced as he stood from his desk.

Mr. Minton turned around and offered his hand in greeting. Sebastian shook it. "Thank you for meeting with us today, Mr. Minton."

"Both of you, please sit down. Can I get you a beverage?" Maxwell asked. Both men declined and took seats opposite Max. "Well, let's get started. Mr. Minton, my brother and I would like to hire you to find our father."

"When was the last time you had contact with him?" Mr. Minton asked, pulling a notepad out of his jacket pocket.

"Twenty-six years ago," Max replied.

"That may prove a little difficult, being so long ago. What can you tell me about him?"

"His name is Martin Christopher Baker," Sebastian began. "I have this photo." Sebastian pulled the photo out of his coat pocket and handed to Mr. Minton.

"Our mother divorced him when she found him cheating on her. I was only ten years of age and Sebastian wasn't born yet, so I'm not sure how much information we can provide," Maxwell jumped in to explain.

Minton nodded as he scribbled away in his notebook. "Do you know of any places he liked to frequent? I need a starting point."

"He met my mother at the Blakesfield Country Club. It was a whirlwind courtship and they married quickly. I don't recall meeting his parents or siblings. I know it's not much to go on," Max apologized.

"Has your mother given you any hints over the years?"

"She won't speak of him. That's why we contacted you. We need this done discreetly."

"Of course. Let me start with public records: birth certificate, divorce decree. Maybe I can pull your mother's financial records to see if she's made any payments to him over the years."

Sebastian looked to Max, who silently nodded his head in agreement. "We would appreciate any information you could gather, Mr. Minton."

Minton reached into his suit coat pocket and produced two business cards. He handed one each to the siblings. "Give me some time to see what I can come up with. I'll keep you informed. My number is on the card if you need to reach me or if you remember anything that will assist me in the search." He shook hands with both men and then he left the office.

Sebastian wasn't sure what he expected from the meeting, but it certainly wasn't Mr. Minton's quick, no-nonsense demeanor. He scratched his head, then headed to the sideboard and poured himself a scotch. "Do you think it is possible she's still paying off father to stay away?"

Maxwell sat in his chair and pondered the question for a long moment. "If she's paying him off, it would explain why he's never tried to contact me."

"Well, I guess we just wait and see now," Sebastian agreed, sitting down in the chair and sipping his scotch.

Max sighed as he shuffled the papers in front of him. "I'm really not in the mood to deal with charities today." He looked at his watch and noted the time was just eleven forty-five. "Why don't we go to my club for lunch?"

Mattie was with Sigourney, so Sebastian didn't need to rush home. "All right, let's go."

~ ~ ~ ~

Sigourney and Mattie paid a visit to Penny. They sat in the parlor drinking tea and eating cucumber sandwiches.

Mattie looked at Sigourney and then turned her attention to Penny. She sat quietly, as if deep in thought, and then asked: "Are you and Uncle Max going to get married?"

"Mattie!" Penny exclaimed. "Whatever gave you that idea?"

"Mummy and I talk about it. We want you to have a boyfriend."

Penny put her hand over her heart, speechless at the child's sweet response.

"Is Max your boyfriend?" Sigourney played along with Mattie.

"It's early days, I don't know how to define it," Penny admitted.

"Have you gone out?" Sigourney asked, creeping to the edge of her seat.

"He has escorted me to charity balls."

"He's come to have tea with Aunt Penny, too," Mattie added.

"And we may have gone on the occasional dinner," Penny admitted with an impish grin.

"Have you kissed?" Mattie inquired.

"Mattie, that's not polite to ask," Penny chided.

"Oh, come now, it's just us girls! Fess up, Pen."

Lowering her eyelids and blushing she whispered, "Yes, we've kissed."

"Don't boyfriends and girlfriends get married?" Mattie asked.

Sigourney grinned. "Sometimes they do."

"Please, I don't want to jinx it," Penny pleaded.

"What does that mean?" Mattie asked looking back and forth between Sigourney and Penny.

"It means that if you say it aloud, it might never happen," Penny explained.

~ ~ ~ ~

Maxwell's private car chauffeured the men to Soho. They entered the dark club, full of rich wood paneling and plush green carpets. An attendant greeted them. "Earl Sutton, it's a pleasure to have to back again."

"Thank you, Marcus. This is my brother, Sebastian. We'd like a table for lunch, please."

"Right this way, my Lord." Marcus escorted them to a prime table in the center of the room—one where you could see everything and be seen. Marcus left the table and Sebastian began to chuckle as he took his seat.

"What has you so amused?" Max inquired with suspicion.

"'My Lord'—I'm sorry, it's just been a very long time since I've been around all this pomp and circumstance."

Max joined in with laughter. "It *does* take some getting used to. This could have all been yours if you were born first," he reminded.

"Well, thank God for small favors." Sebastian looked over the menu. "What are you having?"

"Steak—rare."

"I think I've have the veal."

It was a relaxing meal. Sebastian and Max talked and were becoming more comfortable in each other's presence. When their meal was consumed, they joined the other club members in the smoking room to enjoy a brandy.

Sebastian relaxed into the maroon leather tall-backed chair and inhaled the smell of cigarettes. It had been years since he last smoked, but sometimes the scent made him crave it—especially after a good meal. He observed the room: some members were reading newspapers, some were in deep quiet conversation, and others sat alone drinking. Someone familiar entered the room. He walked down the carpeted steps and stopped in his tracks when his eyes locked with Sebastian's. A smile curled up on the man's handsome face as he set course in Sebastian's direction.

"Bloody hell, Irons. What brings you to London?" Prince Alistair asked, stopping in front of him.

Sebastian stood from the chair and held out his hand. "Blue blood, it is good to see you again. My family recently moved back. My wife has a job with the Associated Press here in London."

"Family—wife? By God, we have a lot to catch up on." Alistair looked at Maxwell. "Earl Sutton, it's good to see you again."

Maxwell stood from his chair. "Your Royal Highness, it's always a pleasure. You are welcome to join us."

"I would love to. However, I have a meeting." Alistair reached into his pocket to pull out a calling card. He handed it to Sebastian. "Please ring me later. I'd love to catch up."

Sebastian nodded in agreement. "I'll do that."

Alistair left the pair and headed toward the back of the room.

"How do you get away with calling him blue blood?" Max wondered, taking his seat.

"I roomed with him at Eton. We've had some interesting adventures together," Sebastian explained, but declined to go into detail. "He must not be aware that you're seeing Penelope Stanton. If he was, I don't know that he'd be so gracious."

"He dated her years ago. He's had ample opportunity to rekindle the relationship if he chose to do so," Max replied.

"Penny doesn't forgive cheaters. Be warned," he clipped out.

"I have no intentions of cheating on Penny."

"Good."

"It's rather endearing how protective you are of the women in your life. I admire that quality in you."

Sebastian was taken aback by the revelation. Unsure how to respond, he took the last sip of his brandy. Finally he muttered, "Thank you, Max."

Sebastian made Mattie her favorite dish, macaroni and cheese, and put her to bed at eight o'clock. Tess had phoned ahead saying she had a deadline and wouldn't be home until late that night. To fill the time, he tried to read a novel, but his mind was too full of information to concentrate on the written words in front of him. Sighing, he closed the book and lay back on the couch. Whatever had made him think he could quietly move his family back to London and go about his business unknown? Ever since stepping foot back in his homeland, he'd been greeted with the ghosts of his past. It seemed as if he were living in a Charles Dickens' novel.

He heard the key turn in the lock and sat up to find Tess walking through the front door. She was the consummate professional: dressed in a light gray suit, her hair pulled up into a chignon, briefcase in hand.

"Hello, darling," he announced, rushing over to greet her with a passionate kiss.

Tess teetered on her heels. "Wow, miss me that much?"

"You have no idea," he replied. "I made a light salad, if you want to eat."

"Oh, that sounds perfect. Could you open a bottle of wine while I get changed and check on Mattie?"

Sebastian confirmed her request by kissing her on the forehead. He busied himself in the kitchen while Tess changed out of her suit. He lit a taper candle and placed her salad and wine on the dining table. Tess came back dressed in her blue silk robe, her hair flowing over her shoulders. She was beautiful and Sebastian would never tire of looking at his wife.

"So how did things go with investigator?" she asked before taking a bite of her salad.

"Okay, I suppose. I mean it's not as if I expected him to say, 'I can find your father in twenty-four hours.' Unfortunately, we didn't have much information to give him. He has to find a paper trail.

I don't know how long it will take or if he'll even find anything."

"And how did things go with Max?"

"Things are getting easier in our relationship. He took me to his club for lunch. I ran into Alistair Windsor."

Tess hadn't heard that name in a long time. Her curiosity was piqued and she raised an eyebrow. "What's up with him?"

"He said I should ring him to catch up. He was surprised I had a family."

"Considering what you two used to do when you hung out together, can you blame him for being surprised?"

"No, I can't blame him. It was odd being in between Penny's ex-flame and current one, though."

"You slept with her, too. So technically all three of you were paramours." Tess grinned. "So are you going to meet up with him?"

"I don't know."

"You changed—maybe Alistair has, too."

"How was your day?" he asked, changing the subject.

"Good. My boss has been so happy with my articles, he wants to send me to Paris next week to cover a story."

"That's great news! I'm so proud of you. When do you leave?"

"Wednesday night. Come with me, Bas. We can spend the weekend in Paris. I had such a wonderful time there on our honeymoon."

Sebastian reached over and took her hand. "I would love that, but what about Mattie?"

"Don't be mad, but when my boss asked me to go I called Penny and asked if she wouldn't mind taking Mattie. She was more than happy to say yes. They'll spend the weekend at the castle with Max."

All Sebastian could do was chuckle. "I really don't know if Penny understands what she agreed to, but I'm game. I certainly would love a romantic weekend with you."

Tess reached over the table and kissed her husband. "Thank you!"

# Chapter 11 - Take Me, I'm Yours

Sebastian and Mattie rode to Penny's townhouse in a black cab. When they arrived at their destination, Sebastian paid the cab driver and then took Mattie's suitcase and stepped out onto the sidewalk while holding his daughter's hand. Mattie ran up to the familiar red door and knocked. Sebastian reached for the doorbell.

Penny opened the door with a warm smile and Mattie jumped into her arms.

"Well, hello, you two," Penny beamed, hugging the child.

Sebastian leaned in and kissed Penny's cheek. "Thanks for taking her this weekend."

"The pleasure is all mine."

"When is Uncle Max picking us up?" Mattie asked impatiently.

"He should come around in about an hour."

Sebastian knelt down in front of his daughter. "Martha, be on your best behavior this weekend. I'll know if you aren't and you won't be permitted to stay with Aunt Penny again."

The child let out a heavy sigh. "Daddy, I'm always good." She then looked up at Penny for confirmation. Penny simply laughed.

Sebastian hugged Mattie and kissed her goodbye. "Ring me at the hotel if you need anything, Pen."

"We'll be fine. Go have a wonderful weekend with your wife!"

Sebastian sat on the Tube heading back to St. John's Wood, studying his fellow riders. It was a constant source of fascination to him. You could observe people from all walks of life: businessmen in their suits and ties, mothers holding babies in their arms, an elderly woman with her grocery shopping, young lovers standing close and whispering in each other's ears. He never would have noticed any of these things if it weren't for Tess. The writer in her was compelled to take in all these little details and she naturally shared them with him, unwittingly turning him into the observer he was today.

The train pulled into the station. The prerecorded message played on the PA system: "Please mind the gap." The riders filed out onto the busy platform and made their way toward the exit.

Walking along the tree-lined street, he reveled in the bright, gorgeous summer afternoon. He was going to spend four days in the City of Love with his amazing, wife and he was heady with anticipation.

Sebastian opened the door to the flat to find Tess grabbing a Coke out of the refrigerator. "Hey, Bas," she greeted.

"You're home early," he said, coming up behind her and planting a kiss on her neck.

"Yes, my boss said I could leave early to pack. Did you get Mattie to Penny's okay?"

"Yes, they both seemed very eager for their weekend in the country."

"I put the suitcases on the bed. Let's go pack. I'm so excited. I can't believe we're going back to Paris!"

The sun was setting as Sebastian and Tess arrived at their hotel, just a few blocks away from the Eiffel Tower. The bellman collected their luggage while the couple walked up to the front desk to check in. "Monsieur et Madam, bienvenue!"

"Merci beaucoup," Sebastian rattled off without thought.

Tess glanced over at her husband and smiled as he and the desk clerk continued their polite conversation in French. She watched as the clerk handed over the room key and motioned for the bellman to take their luggage to the room.

After the bags were delivered, the bellman left them to the comfort of their accommodation. It was modern and elegantly decorated, nothing like the ornateness of the George V. The AP was footing the bill, so Tess couldn't complain. The room did have a lovely view of the Seine River.

"I can't believe I have you to all to myself for four days," Sebastian murmured, walking up behind his wife and wrapping his arms around her waist.

"Speak to me in French," she requested, leaning into her husband.

"Je'taime, mon chéri."

Tess closed her eyes and sighed. "You turn me on when you speak in different languages."

"I thought everything about me turns you on," he teased, nipping her ear with his teeth.

Tess turned around and kissed Sebastian—a sweet, soft kiss. Then the kiss deepened, turning feral and desperate. They spent so much time these days working and raising Mattie, there seemed to be little time for just the two of them. Well, not tonight—

Sebastian would see to that. He picked Tess up off the floor and carried her over to the king-sized bed, gently laying her on top of the luxurious ivory, silk duvet. Her long brown hair fanned out on the pillow, and the top few buttons on her blouse popped open to reveal her cleavage. Sebastian teased her by running his fingers along the swell of breast on view for him.

Sebastian closed his eyes and inhaled her scent while various things he wanted to do to her body raced through his mind. He reached for her waist and pulled down the zipper of her navy skirt. She lifted her hips and shimmied the fabric down her legs. Next, Sebastian unbuttoned her silk blouse. It fell away to reveal her black, lacy demi-bra. Tess sat up and removed the blouse and then reached around her back to unhook the bra. It was carelessly thrown on the floor as she put her arms around his neck and pulled him back down on top of her. His hand ran over her panties and felt she was wet and ready to take him. "I want you so badly," he growled, kissing her with force.

"Take me, I'm yours," she replied in a breathy, seductive tone of voice.

Sebastian pushed away from his wife and stood to remove his clothes. The action done with such haste, a cuff link went flying across the room and bounced off the lamp. His lust-filled eyes roamed over her curves. Soon he was back on the bed, kissing her feet and working his way up her legs until he reached the sweet spot he so wanted to delve into. Removing the delicate lacy fabric, he licked his lips and began to work her into a frenzy with his tongue. Tess squirmed under this touch, eager for more. Just as she was about to climax, Sebastian pulled back.

"No," she whimpered, reaching out for his body, mourning the loss of his tongue on her.

Sebastian took the tip of his erection and guided it to her folds. With one swift motion, he was inside her: hard, quick, and fast. The sudden movement sent Tess over the edge. Feeling her body orgasm did Sebastian in and he soon followed suit—happy, sated, and in love.

"I will never tire of being with you like this," he said between ragged breaths. "I love you."

"I love you, Bas," she whispered, running her fingers through his hair as he laid his head on her shoulder.

"I could use a nap," he yawned.

"And then some room service so we can do this again," Tess added.

"Most definitely."

They slept for an hour and then ordered room service. Happily sitting in bed, noshing on French crepes and fresh fruit, Tess looked over at Sebastian. "I wonder how Max and Penny are doing with Mattie."

"They have our number if they need to reach us. Mattie should be asleep by now."

"I think things are pretty serious between Max and Penny."

"I don't want to talk about them, darling. I just want to concentrate on you," Sebastian said, taking the tray of food away from Tess and placing it on the floor.

"Hmm, you'll get no argument from me," she purred, wrapping her naked body around his.

"What time is your interview tomorrow?"

"Ten o'clock," she replied, kissing his chest.

"Good, then I have all night to make love to you."

# Chapter 12 - Be My Wife

Mattie was dressed in her fancy pink dress, the one with all the ruffles on the skirt. She sat at the dinner table with Max and Penny, eating an early supper. "Can I ride the pony tomorrow?" she asked her uncle.

"Yes, we can ride tomorrow."

"Awesome!"

Penny chuckled at the child's enthusiasm. "Don't you miss your mum and dad, Mattie?"

"No, I love coming to the castle. I wish I could live here."

Now Maxwell joined in the chuckling. "You're welcome here anytime."

"Mattie, if you're finished your meal, you should get ready for bed. The pony will be up bright and early tomorrow morning, so you must be ready."

Thankfully, the mention of the pony was all that was needed to convince Mattie it was bedtime. "May

I be excused?" Mattie politely asked, looking at Maxwell.

"Yes, you may be excused," he replied, touching her little hand.

Penny and the child stood from the table and made their way upstairs.

Once they were inside the nursery, Mattie changed into her pajamas and crawled under the covers. "Will you read me a story like Daddy does every night?"

"Certainly. What would you like to read?" Penny asked, walking over to the bookshelf filled with children's books.

"Paddington Bear."

"Ah, this is a good one," Penny said, pulling a copy of *Paddington Abroad* by Michael Bond from the shelf.

Penny sat down on the bed and began to read the book. In the story, Mr. Brown decides the family should take a vacation to Paris and Paddington is given a beret and French phrase book. Fifteen minutes into the story, Mattie was sound asleep.

Maxwell was watching the two interact, quietly hanging back in the hallway. Penny closed the book and laid it on the bedside table. "You're wonderful with her," he whispered, padding into the room and placing his hand on Penny's shoulder.

"She's a joy, Max. Sebastian and Tess are so lucky to have her."

Maxwell got down on one knee, pulling a small box from his tuxedo jacket. He slowly opened the velvet box to reveal a five-carat emerald cut diamond flanked by two baguettes set in platinum. "Penelope, I know we haven't been together for a very long time, but I love you and I want to marry you. Will you have me?"

Penny let out an audible gasp at the sight of the ring and Max kneeling before her. She threw caution to the wind and wrapped her arms around his neck. "Yes! I will marry you, Maxwell. I love you, too."

Beaming with joy, Max slipped the ring on her finger. He pulled her up from the bed, picked her up in his arms, and carried her from Mattie's bedroom.

Penny lay in Maxwell's arms after they made love. She couldn't take her eyes off the ring he had given her a few hours earlier. "Happy?" he asked, pulling her closer.

"Stunned, elated, ecstatic. You've made the happiest girl in England. This ring—I have no words."

"I'm glad you like it. It's a family heirloom. It was my grandmother's engagement ring," he explained.

"You've given me the Countess' ring. Oh, Max," she smiled at him, tears threatening to spill over onto her cheeks.

"So, when do you want to get married? I vote for sooner rather than later."

Penny nodded in agreement. "I would like to get married as soon as possible."

"Westminster Abbey or St. Paul's?"

"Neither," Penny quickly answered. "They'll be booked for months."

"I am an earl, I can pull some strings."

"Let's get married here at the castle. Sebastian and Tess' wedding was at their home in America. It was an intimate, romantic affair. I want that, Max."

"But, love, I'm an earl and you come from a prominent family. I don't think we can get away with a small affair. However, I do love the idea of having the ceremony here. God knows there's enough room."

Penny grinned with joy. "I can pull it together in two months."

"You can find a dress that quickly?"

"My parents own a department store. I have connections, too."

Max leaned in and kissed her full on the lips, savoring her scent and taste. "September it is. You've made me the happiest man on earth."

"Trying to one-up me already, my Lord?" she teased, planting a light kiss on his chest.

"I mean it. I love you, Penelope Stanton. I can't wait to marry you and raise a family."

"I can't wait, either."

Mattie was still sleeping at eight thirty in the morning. Max and Penny decided to wake her from her slumber. The child rolled over on her back and rubbed the sleep from her eyes. When she noticed Max was holding a large white box with a pink satin ribbon, she quickly sat up. "Is that a present for me?"

"Yes, would you like to open it?"

She nodded her head furiously. Max set the box on her lap and Mattie pulled the end of the ribbon until it unraveled in her hand. She lifted the edge of the box and looked inside. Under the white tissue paper, there was a riding outfit: red jacket, white shirt, khaki jodhpurs, and black leather riding boots. "It's just like Daddy's outfit! Can I go on the fox hunt, too?"

"You're a little young for that yet. Maybe once you become a more experienced rider," Max said.

"Come on, let's get you dressed and we'll have some breakfast before we ride," Penny said, removing the box from Mattie's lap. "Max, we'll meet you downstairs." Penny leaned in and gave Max an affectionate kiss.

Mattie giggled and Max winked at her before he turned and left the room. It was then that Mattie noticed the large diamond ring on Penny's finger. She grabbed Penny's hand to get a closer look. "Wow."

"Can you keep a secret?" Penny whispered, sitting down on the bed next to Mattie.

"Yes."

"Uncle Max asked me to marry him last night."

"Yay! Can I come to the wedding?"

"How would you like to be *in* the wedding as our flower girl?"

"Awesome!" Mattie threw herself at Penny and gave her a big hug.

# Chapter 13 - Maybe I'm Amazed

Sebastian and Tess' flight landed at Heathrow Airport at six o'clock Sunday night. They made their way to Penny's townhouse to collect Mattie before they headed for home. Mattie noticed her parents, as they walked into the room hand in hand. She ran over to greet them. After hugs and kisses were exchanged, Mattie stood before Tess bouncing up and down on the tips of her toes, excitement sparkling in her baby blue eyes.

"What's got you so excited?" Sebastian asked.

Mattie held her mouth shut, her arms moving up and down.

"Mattie, what's going on?"

Mattie remained silent but looked back at Max and Penny, who were standing nearby. Max had his arm around Penny's shoulder. Tess looked up at the couple and noticed the light glance off the huge rock on Penny's finger. Tess rushed over to Penny and picked up her hand. "Oh my God, is this what I think it is?"

Before Penny could respond, Mattie shouted, "They're getting married!"

"Congratulations! Penny, this ring is spectacular. I'm so happy for you both." The women hugged and then Tess leaned over and kissed Max on the cheek. "This is wonderful news."

Sebastian walked toward the happy couple. "Well, at least you have good taste in women." He extended his hand to Max. "Congratulations."

Max refused to take his brother's hand, instead pulling him into a hug. "We have your blessing, then?" Max said in a low tone of voice as the girls chatted over them.

Sebastian nodded. "If you truly love her—yes, you have my blessing. What does Lily think?"

"We haven't told her yet. You and Tess are the first."

"Max, we must open a bottle of champagne!" Penny announced.

Max rushed off to the kitchen. Penny walked over to Sebastian and hugged him.

"Are you happy, Pen?" Sebastian asked.

"I've never been more happy in my life," she replied.

Sebastian squeezed her tightly. "I'm so happy for you. You'll make a beautiful bride."

Soon Max was back with a bottle of champagne and a white grape juice for Mattie. They toasted Max and Penny's upcoming nuptials and talked about wedding plans and Sebastian and Tess' trip to Paris. By eight o'clock, Mattie was tired. She rested her head on Sebastian's lap.

"Too much excitement this weekend. I think we better get her home to bed," Sebastian said, glancing over at his wife.

Tess nodded in agreement and everyone stood to say their goodbyes. She grabbed Mattie's suitcase while Sebastian scooped his daughter up in his arms. Max and Penny waved farewell standing in the open doorway of the townhouse as the family got into a cab to head home.

Her daughter barely moved as Tess took off her dress and put Mattie in her pajamas. Sebastian tucked her into bed and turned out the light. "Maybe we should give her to Max and Penny more often if they can wear her out like this," he mused as he and Tess walked to their bedroom.

"I'm so happy they like her," Tess admitted as she began to undress. "I never could have imagined she'd transition to the move this well."

"You've done a fine job yourself," Sebastian complimented as he tossed his tie and shirt over the chair. He walked over to his wife, pulled her into an embrace, and gave her a sweet and tender kiss.

"A wedding—isn't it wonderful? Penny will get her happy ending, too," Tess sighed, leaning into Sebastian's bare chest.

"It's very quick, but I believe Max truly loves her and Penny seems over the moon, so why not have a wedding?" he conceded.

"Gee, if you could show any more enthusiasm, I just might die," she teased.

"I'm English. I don't show enthusiasm," Sebastian warned.

"Nonsense! I've seen your enthusiasm in our bed," she replied, pulling him toward the mattress.

"Oh, well, that's a different matter altogether," he smirked as he fell on top of her and kissed her.

In the morning, Sebastian made scrambled eggs and toast for his girls. Tess finished her plate and gave kisses to her husband and daughter before setting off to work. Once he and Mattie were alone, she asked, "What shall we do today, Daddy?"

"I don't know, love. What were you thinking?"

"Let's go shopping and buy Uncle Max and Aunt Penny a present."

"What type a present?"

"Something romantic."

"What do you know about romance?" Sebastian inquired, yet again amazed at the young girl's vocabulary.

"Romance is kissing. You and Mummy are always kissing."

"That's because I love your mummy very much."

"Uncle Max and Aunt Penny are in love, too."

"So it appears they are." Sebastian stood from the table and reached for Mattie's breakfast plate. "Why don't you go get dressed and we'll head over to Fortum and Mason and see what we can find?"

"Yay! Can we have tea there, too?"

"You're turning into a regular English lass, aren't you?" he grinned. "Get going."

Sebastian cleaned the dirty dishes and glanced at the card that Alistair had given him last week, which was sitting on the counter. He'd been contemplating giving Alistair a call, but wasn't sure if it was the right thing to do. He was too old to get involved in the mayhem they used to live. Actually, it wasn't his age but his maturity that prevented him from wanting to get involved in that lifestyle again. Alistair was still the darling of the gossip papers—currently dating a very tall, leggy, blonde, South African model.

Mattie walked back into the room wearing a blue cotton dress and her black Mary Jane shoes, and carrying a small purse that Penny had bought her. "I'm ready."

"You look very lovely today, Mattie," her father observed. "Why aren't you wearing jeans?"

"Daddy, we're going to tea. I have to dress properly."

Sebastian chuckled to himself as he grabbed his suit jacket from the back of the kitchen chair. "Off we go, then."

They walked into Fortum and Mason at 181 Piccadilly, the three-hundred-year-old store looking bright and inviting. Mattie walked over to the sweets counter and marveled at the various confectionary treats. "We should get some chocolate for Mummy," she said, looking up at Sebastian.

"Yes, she would like that, wouldn't she? Let's go upstairs and find Aunt Penny's gift first." He guided Mattie up the stairs to the first floor of the department store, where the cook shop, china, and silver were displayed.

Mattie wandered about with great fascination, Sebastian by her side. Finally, she stopped in front of a table of picture frames. "I like that one," she said, pointing at an eight by ten ornate floral sterling frame.

Sebastian picked it up to inspect it closer. "You really like this one?"

"Yes, they can put their wedding picture in it."

"I think it's a fine gift."

The sales associate rang up the sale and gift-wrapped the frame for them. Mattie insisted on carrying the light green shopping bag as they took the lift to The Fountain restaurant for tea. They sat at a table for two near the window. Sebastian placed their order then turned to his daughter. "So tell me about your weekend at the castle."

"Uncle Max bought me an outfit to ride my pony."

"I don't think it's your pony, darling."

"Uncle Max said it was."

"I think you love Uncle Max more than you love me," he playfully pouted.

Mattie got down from her chair and walked over to Sebastian and hugged him. "I love you more than anyone in the world, Daddy."

He leaned down and kissed the top of her head. It had been a long time since he'd heard that phrase. It brought back wonderful memories of Nanny Jones. "And I you, Mattie."

# Chapter 14 - Lost And Found

Sebastian sat in Maxwell's office waiting for Mr. Minton to arrive. It had been two weeks since his last meeting with the investigator, and Sebastian wasn't sure what to expect. He sat quietly in a chair, his left leg bouncing up and down in anticipation.

There was a knock, followed by Max's assistant opening the door and announcing Mr. Minton. Both Sebastian and his brother stood to greet the investigator.

"Please, have a seat," Mr. Minton announced. He sat down and pulled a file from his briefcase, opened it, and looked over the notes. Sebastian wished he'd just cut to the chase. "I was able to confirm your father, Martin Christopher Baker, was born in Brixton. He was an only child of Nancy and Stuart Baker—both deceased. Mr. Baker did work for the Country Club in the late fifties, where he met your mother. After they married, he moved into your country estate. He didn't hold down a job. You and your sister Victoria were born a year after the wedding."

"Do you know where he is today? Is he even alive?" Sebastian anxiously inquired.

"I wasn't able to find a death certificate. I did find proof that your mother has been making yearly payments to him over the past twenty-five years."

"Through a London bank?" Max asked.

Mr. Minton grimaced. "No, it's through a Swiss bank account. The account is active, so I believe Mr. Baker is still alive."

"Can it be traced?"

"I'm working on it. It won't be easy. I just wanted to keep you abreast of the situation."

Max extended his hand to the investigator. "Thank you, Mr. Minton."

"I'm sorry I don't have more information. The search is proving to be more difficult than I anticipated."

"You're running into dead ends. That isn't your fault," Sebastian told him.

"If your father can be found, I'll be sure to find him," Minton reassured.

Then Mr. Minton was gone. Sebastian and Maxwell looked at each other. Sebastian exhaled loudly.

"You really didn't expect him to come back in a few weeks and say he found him?" Max asked.

"I suppose not," Sebastian said. "I need a drink."

"The club?"

"Yes."

They sat in the corner of the quiet room, sipping scotch and discussing the whereabouts of their father. "I can broach the subject with Mother, but I can't promise anything," Max suggested.

"She won't tell you anything, I know that for a fact."

"Nothing ventured, nothing gained."

"Have you told her about your engagement?"

"Yes," Max clipped out.

Sebastian chuckled to himself. He couldn't help it. "I take it she wasn't very pleased."

"She thinks I can do better. I disagree."

"Christ, how many virginal socialites does she think still exist?" Sebastian muttered.

"I don't care what she thinks. I choose Penelope."

"I think it's the best decision you've ever made."

"She's pulling together an engagement party next weekend. Will you come?"

"Will Lily be there?"

"I don't know," Max honestly replied. "She's been invited. I don't care if she comes or not."

"If she's there, I won't attend." Sebastian looked down at this Rolex. "I've got to get going."

"Sebastian, please don't be like this."

Sebastian stood and looked at Max. "Like what? Don't pass judgment on me until you've had a family of your own. Maybe then you'll understand the lengths you'll go to in order to protect them."

"You're right," Max softly admitted, making eye contact with his brother.

Sebastian nodded. "I'll ring you later." He turned on his heel and left the room. As he walked down the marble hall to the vestibule, be bumped into Alistair.

"Sebastian, you didn't ring me. We should get together."

"Sorry, Tess got called out of town on business. I took the trip with her to Paris. Why don't you come over to dinner—say Friday at seven o'clock? You can meet my family."

"I'd love it. What's the address?"

"Seventy-Five St. Edmunds Terrace, St. John's Wood."

"I'll see you then," Alistair agreed, clapping him on the back.

*It's been one hell of day,* Sebastian thought to himself as he laid his head on the pillow. Tess curled her arms around him and he let out an audible sigh. "I'm happy this day is over," he admitted and then kissed her softly on the lips.

"I'm sure the investigator is doing everything in his power to find your father. I understand it must be torture to wait."

"I'm not even sure that's what's troubling me."

"What else happened?"

"I saw Alistair at the club and invited him to dinner on Friday. I hope that's okay," he slowly replied, hoping not to upset his wife.

"It's been years since you've seen him. You changed, maybe he has too."

"I reckon it's possible. We'll find out Friday night."

"What do I wear to meet a prince?"

"Wear your jeans and sweatshirt and I'll get takeaway from McDonalds," he joked.

Tess playfully slapped his ass. "I'm serious. I don't want to do the wrong thing."

"Darling, we're eating here. We are not going to the palace. I'll make a nice dinner. It will be relaxed and casual."

"I'll be sure to get home on time. My boss will flip when I tell him I'm having dinner with a member of the Royal Family."

"Don't get too excited. It's just Alistair."

"I think it's exciting! Aren't you looking forward to it?"

"I don't know, Tess. I have too much on my mind lately."

She looked at him with concern. "Something else is bothering you, isn't it?"

"Max wants us to go to the engagement party."

"Well, of course we'll go. Why does that bother you?"

"Lily."

Tess' expression fell serious. "I didn't think about that."

"Exactly."

"She can't hurt us, Bas. We've got each other's backs. She only has the power if we give it to her."

He smiled at his beautiful, strong girl. *God, how I love her.* "What about Mattie? I want to protect her."

"You *do* protect her. We'll keep her away from Lily. We have to go to the party. Penny's one of your oldest and dearest friends and Max is your brother. Let's show Lily just how great our lives are without her," Tess finished with conviction.

"I love you," he whispered, placing his hand behind her neck and pulling her in for a wonderfully long kiss.

# Chapter 15 - Prince Charming

The doorbell of the Irons household rang promptly at seven o'clock. Sebastian opened the door to find Alistair dressed in a bespoke navy suit, crisp white shirt, and red striped tie. He was holding a bottle of wine in his hand. "Good evening," he greeted.

"Alistair, please come in," Sebastian said, standing aside to allow his guest entrance to his home.

Tess stood a few feet away, dressed in her Calvin Klein and black heels. Mattie, who was wearing her prettiest pink frock, held her hand. Alistair walked forward and greeted Tess. She curtsied with a blush.

"Tess, you don't need to curtsy. You're not English."

"I'm sorry. I've never met a prince before. I don't know the protocol."

Alistair laughed. "Please—just call me Alistair. Sebastian never once called me by my title. I don't expect his wife to, either." He looked down at Mattie and smiled. "And who do we have here?"

Mattie politely bowed and then offered her hand. "I'm Mattie Irons."

Alistair took the child's hand and shook it. "Pleasure to meet you, Mattie Irons."

"Can I call you Uncle Alistair?"

"Martha, you've only just met," Sebastian admonished.

"Yes, you can call me Uncle Alistair." He winked at the little girl.

"Come, dinner is ready," Sebastian announced, escorting the group to the dining room. "No servants tonight, blue blood. Take a seat."

Alistair sat in one of the four chairs at the round table, which was dressed with the family's best linens and china. Mattie sat next to him. Sebastian and Tess went into the kitchen to bring out the food. Soon they were eating a meal of veal with roasted potatoes, steamed broccoli, and green beans.

"This is delicious. My compliments to the chief," Alistair said, nodding toward Tess.

Tess giggled and then said, "You'll have to thank Sebastian. He's the cook in the family."

"Surely, you're pulling my leg."

"It's true," Sebastian confirmed. "Much has transpired since we said our goodbyes."

"Where do you work?" Mattie asked.

"Well, Mattie, I have a job in the Royal Navy. I fly helicopters."

"Cool," she replied before taking a bite of her veal.

"Yes, it's very cool," he agreed. "How did you get to be so adorable?"

"Mummy says I take after my daddy," she replied in all seriousness.

"Your father always was the charmer."

"What does that mean?"

"That means he was always very polite and everyone liked him."

Over the course of the dinner, Alistair went on to tell the group about his travels to Africa, while Sebastian and Tess talked about living in New Jersey and working in New York. When they finished their meal, Tess put Mattie to bed. Sebastian and Alistair sat in the living room, enjoying an after dinner drink.

"I read in the papers that Penny Stanton and your brother are engaged. That was a surprise," Alistair said, crossing his legs as he sipped his scotch.

"Do you keep in touch with Penny?"

Alistair laughed. "After she told me to sod off and few other choice words—no."

"You cheated on her in public. How did you think she'd react?"

"Irons, you were no saint back then either," Alistair reminded him.

"Yes, I know. Things changed. I met Tess. I have a beautiful daughter. I wouldn't trade that for anything in the world."

Alistair became quiet, lost in thought. Finally, he looked Sebastian in the eye and said, "Penny was the best thing that ever happened to me and I blew it."

"I won't disagree. Why didn't you go after her?"

"I was young and stupid. Hell, we all were back then—all of us except Penny. I was going to the Naval Academy, and it just didn't seem possible to carry on a relationship." Alistair looked down at his perfectly manicured fingernails and asked, "Is she well?"

"Yes, she is well. You can't tell me you never run into her."

"A few times—here and there. She smiles politely, but we never speak."

"And now that you see someone else is serious about her, you want her back?"

"No, she'd never have me even if it were possible. I like Maxwell. He'll be good to her." He placed his glass down on the coffee table and ran his hand through his blond hair. "Bollocks! I'm just feeling sorry for myself."

"Poor Prince Alistair."

"Sod off, Irons," he said, cracking a grin.

The two old friends looked at one another and began laughing aloud. Just then Tess walked back into the room. "Keep it down you two. Mattie just fell asleep," she admonished as she sat down next to Sebastian.

"Sorry, darling," he apologized, kissing her temple.

"So tell me, Tess: what on earth made you fall in love with Sebastian?"

Tess looked up at her husband. Her lips curled up into a smile. "I had never met anyone like him before. He's the most loyal friend I've ever had, the most loving husband, and the best father."

Sebastian looked at her, his eyes shining bright with happiness. "I love you," he whispered, forgetting Alistair was still in the room.

Alistair cleared his throat to get the couple's attention. "I'd best be going. You two lovebirds seem like you need some alone time."

"Please, you're welcome to stay a while longer," Tess offered.

"Thank you for a wonderful dinner." Alistair stood and kissed Tess on the cheek. Next, he shook

Sebastian's hand. "If you'd like, I'd love to have you by Kensington Palace in a few weeks for dinner. I have an apartment there. You're welcome to bring Mattie, too."

"Thank you for the offer, but I'm not sure you want Mattie running around the palace," Sebastian said.

Tess looked up at her husband with expectant eyes. "She would love it and so would I."

"It's settled then. I'll have my secretary ring you next week with a date."

"Thank you, Alistair. It was a pleasure to meet you," Tess said, extending her hand.

Opening the front door, Sebastian said, "Have a good evening." He watched as Alistair made his way to the Range Rover parked in front of their home. When he had driven off, Sebastian loosened his tie and shook his head in disbelief. "How did you mange to wrangle an invitation to the palace?"

"You've known him how many years and you've never been there?" Tess asked in disbelief.

"Back then, the palace—any palace—was the last place we wanted to be." Sebastian took her hand and led her to the bedroom.

"Yes, I suppose wild parties and fine painting and antiques don't mix. Too many things could get broken."

"Exactly."

"He seems nice enough. Do you think he's tamed his wild ways?"

"Maybe he has. It's hard to say. He's regretting letting Penny get away."

"He told you that?"

"Yes." Sebastian closed the bedroom door and began to take off his suit.

"Hmm, interesting time for him to pop back into the picture," Tess mused, stepping out of her dress and then hanging it in the closet.

"I'll keep an eye on him. I don't need him stirring up trouble for Max and Pen."

"I think that's a wise decision," Tess agreed. She pulled down the duvet and got into bed. "I still want to go to dinner at the palace."

"Said the girl who loves McDonald's."

Tess giggled. "How many people do you think get invited by a prince to have dinner in the palace?"

"I had a castle—isn't that enough?" he joked.

"Bas, I want to go and so will Mattie."

"You want to go because the writer in you wants to observe and jot it down for some grandiose tale."

"I write fact, not fiction." She curled up next to her husband as he lay down on the bed. "But maybe someday I might write a novel, and that will be an experience I'll have tucked in the back of my mind."

"Why don't you just ask him for an interview—help him clean up that wild boy image of his?"

"Not a bad idea, Bas. I'll think about it."

"Goodnight, darling."

"Love you."

Two weeks later, they were escorted through the gates of Kensington Palace to have dinner with Alistair. He had a small block of apartments at the back of the property, tucked away from the prying eyes of the public.

"I know this is just another day for you, but I think it's exciting," Tess said in a low tone as they walked down the carpeted hall to meet Alistair. She had worn her Chanel and bought a new pale yellow dress for Mattie, pulling her hair back with a satin ribbon.

Alistair greeted them with a smile. "Welcome to Kensington Palace."

Tess and Mattie both curtsied. Sebastian extended his hand, but Alistair refused the handshake and gave his old friend a manly hug.

"Uncle Alistair, can we see the gardens after dinner?" Mattie asked.

"Of course we can. For now, follow me." They continued down the long, red-carpeted hallway, passing priceless works of art and antiquities. Alistair played tour guide, pointing out various pieces as they walked along.

They sat down to a dinner served by a footman in livery. The food was perfection and no detail was spared. Tess was so proud of Mattie, who behaved like a perfect lady.

"Tess, tell me more about your work with the Associated Press," Alistair asked, placing the linen napkin over his lap.

"It is fast-paced and wonderful. We tend to scour news outlets for stories, rewrite them, and get them out over the wire. On occasion I get sent out on an interview."

"Is there a specific field you work in?"

"I've covered everything from local to global news, political and special interest stories."

"What does a prince do?" Mattie asked.

Sebastian began to chuckle and Alistair gave him a smirk. "I work for the firm."

"What do you do?"

"He's very good and shaking people's hands, cutting ribbons, and smiling for photos," Sebastian jumped in just to give Alistair a good ribbing.

"It's an art I dare say you'd fail at, Irons."

"Undoubtedly."

"I know about the Prince's Trust. Do you have an organization that you patron?" Tess asked.

"Yes, there are a few."

"I didn't know that," Sebastian quipped.

"You haven't been around lately."

"Well, maybe you should focus on the good things you do instead of being fodder for the gossip rags."

"I would love to interview you and talk about those organizations. I'm sure they would love the publicity. We could shine the light on their cause," Tess offered.

Alistair pondered the request for a moment, then said, "I'll give you my private secretary's card. I'm sure we can set something up."

"Thank you."

"Now if everyone is finished with their meal, let's take a walk in the gardens, shall we?"

They trooped out to the private back garden and walked around the grounds as the sun began to set, turning the sky a beautiful palette of blue, pink, and orange. Tess and Mattie walked ahead, leaving Alistair and Sebastian time for a private talk.

"I still can't believe it. You have a family," Alistair remarked, shaking his head in disbelief. "Whatever happened to the Libertines? We were young and foolish and it was grand!"

"We grew up—at least Penny and I did. Not so sure about you, from what I still read in the tabloids." Sebastian stopped to inspect one of the many rose bushes along the garden's path. "Don't you grow weary of the parties and paparazzi?"

"Yes."

"So do something about it. Put the spotlight on the people and organizations that need help. Stop being the playboy," Sebastian urged his friend.

"Like you?"

"I love the life I have with Tess and Mattie. I wouldn't give it up for the world."

"Maybe I just need to find someone to settle down with."

"Someone like Penny?"

"I'm afraid that ship sailed a long time ago," Alistair sighed. "She was mine and I fucked it up. Now it's too late to get her back."

"She's very happy with Maxwell, if that's any consolation," Sebastian chimed in.

"It's no consolation at all."

# Chapter 16 - Celebration

The engagement party for Maxwell and Penelope was held at Max's Mayfair home, just a stone's throw from Buckingham Palace. The house was elegant and imposing—four stories tall, with an ornate facade and slate roof. Sebastian walked his family up the stone steps and rang the doorbell. A butler opened the door to greet them, and they were escorted to the ballroom, where the festivities were already under way.

"Mattie, stay close. There are many people here this evening and I don't want you to get lost," Sebastian warned, still holding the child's hand.

"Where's Uncle Max and Aunt Penny? I want to give them their present."

Just then, the happy couple noticed the Irons family and walked toward them.

"Uncle Max!" Mattie exclaimed, rushing to greet her uncle.

Max picked her up and gave her a hug. "What do we have here?" he asked, noticing the expertly gift-wrapped package she was holding.

"It's my present for you and Aunt Penny."

"Thank you, Mattie," Penny chimed in as she took the gift from Mattie's hand. "We won't open the gifts tonight, but if you would like to come over tomorrow we can open all the presents once everyone is gone."

Mattie looked to her father for approval.

"Yes, we can come by tomorrow."

"Awesome!" Mattie exclaimed.

Max set Mattie back down on the floor. "Thank you for coming tonight," he said to both Sebastian and Tess.

"We wouldn't miss it," Tess said.

"Is she here?" Sebastian needed to know.

"She declined," Maxwell replied.

"Something about me not being up to snuff as an earl's wife, I believe, wasn't it, Max?" Penny asked, making light of situation.

"Not the first time I've heard something like that," Sebastian muttered.

Tess laced her arm through his. "That just means the party will be even better without her."

Sebastian squeezed his wife's hand and smiled. "Let's celebrate."

A waiter stopped nearby with a silver tray of champagne. The four adults each took a glass. "To Max and Pen: may you have a long, adventurous, and loving life together."

"Cheers to that, brother," Max replied as they clinked glasses and took a sip of the marvelous elixir.

Tess knelt down and said to Mattie, "Let's go find you something to drink and then we can sit over on that sofa and look at all the pretty dresses everyone is wearing."

Mattie nodded her head in agreement and she and Tess walked off, leaving Max, Penny, and Sebastian alone.

"Pen, you are the best thing that ever happened to Maxwell. If Lily can't see it, she's the fool."

"I concur," Max said.

"I couldn't care less what Lady Lily Irons thinks of me. I'm happy," she said, looking up at Max. "That's all that matters. And you brought your family to celebrate with us."

"I'll leave you to your guests."

Sebastian made his way to corner of the room, where a small sofa was stationed. He found his family sitting there, observing the crowd. Taking a seat on the arm of the sofa, he said, "So who is winning?"

"I like the lady in the red dress," Mattie said, pointing in the unknown woman's direction.

"I'd say that's a Valentino," Sebastian remarked.

"Is anyone wearing Chanel like Mummy?" Mattie asked.

"Take a look, I'm sure you'll spot someone in time."

Tess chuckled. "You would have to teach her a designer version of *I Spy.*"

Just then, Mattie bounced in her seat and pointed to the opposite side of the room. "Daddy, over there, by the tall vase." The woman she pointed out was wearing a long black off-the-shoulder gown. A silk white camellia flower was pinned to the black satin belt.

"Excellent eye!"

They spent the next hour admiring the partygoers and nibbling on hors d'oeuvres. When the live band began to play music, Mattie and Tess both insisted on dancing. The three of them made their way to the dance floor, Sebastian holding Mattie in one arm and wrapping his free arm around Tess.

"This is nice. Aren't you glad we came?" Tess asked as they swayed to the music.

"I am," Mattie jumped in.

"Me, too," Sebastian agreed.

"Daddy, can you put me down? I want to dance by myself."

Sebastian complied with her request and the child took both her parents' hands and moved in time with the music. He was grateful to put her down, because she was getting too heavy to hold. His little girl was growing up way too fast. In a few weeks' time, she would start school. He was sure he'd miss her like the devil, and started to think about having a second child. Tess wouldn't go for it—at least not until she was able to get herself established in the London office at the Associated Press. There was also the continuing search for his father and Max and Penny's upcoming nuptials—too many things to be contemplating another child at this point in time.

"Hey, what were you thinking about?" Tess asked as she caressed his cheek.

Sebastian pressed his lips to the palm of her hand. "Nothing—just happy to be here with my girls."

"Mummy, I want some strawberries," Mattie said, tugging on her mother's hand.

"Okay, let's see if we can find some."

"I can take her," Sebastian offered.

"I got it. Go dance with Penny."

Sebastian nodded his head in agreement and walked over to Maxwell and Penny, who were dancing in the center of the room. Sebastian tapped Max's shoulder to cut in. His brother graciously stepped back and Sebastian took Penny into his arms. "Quite a turnout," he said, looking around at the crowd as they danced to the music.

"In five weeks, I'll be Mrs. Maxwell Irons," she smiled.

"You look very happy."

"I am."

"It doesn't bother you that Lily isn't here?"

"It's her loss."

"More like our gain," he muttered. "How's Max taking it?"

"It doesn't seem to faze him in the least."

"Good."

"Do you know how adorable it is that you are so protective of your family?"

"Adorable? I take offense to that," he cringed.

"You're right—a Libertine would never be adorable," she teased.

Sebastian laughed aloud. He thought back to the time he, Alistair, and Penny got the tattoos. "What does Max think about the tattoo?"

"He's glad it's only visible when I'm naked," she said in a low voice so no one would hear.

"I bet you'll be the first countess with a tattoo. How scandalous!"

Before she could respond, Maxwell tapped the sleeve of Sebastian's tuxedo. "You've monopolized my fiancée long enough. Step aside, little brother."

"Yes, my Lord," he mocked as he stepped away from Penny. Sebastian looked around the room. He spotted his girls by the dessert table and walked over to join them.

Mattie was leaning against Tess, her eyes heavy with sleep. "I think we should get her home, Bas. It's getting late," Tess said.

Sebastian scooped Mattie up into his arms, and the little girl nuzzled her head onto his shoulder. A small yawn escaped her lips. "I'm tired, Daddy."

"I know, love. Let's go home."

# Chapter 17 - State of Shock

Sebastian placed a bowl of cereal and a slice of toast on the table in front of Mattie. "Eat up. It's your first day of school."

"Aren't you excited?" Tess asked, sipping her tea.

"I don't want to go to school. I want to stay with Daddy," she pouted.

"I have to go to the gallery, darling. You'll love school. You'll get to meet new friends."

"Wouldn't you like to have other little girls to play with?" Tess asked.

Mattie shrugged her shoulders and placed a spoonful of cereal in her mouth. Maybe she wasn't like Tess after all, Sebastian mused. He sat down next to her and looked her in the eyes. "You're just nervous, but you'll see all the children will feel the same way you do, and in no time you'll have a group of new friends."

After they finished their breakfast, Sebastian placed the dirty dishes in the dishwasher. Tess knelt down in front of her daughter and inspected her school uniform. It was a navy plaid skirt and white shirt with a Peter Pan collar. She was wearing white knee socks and saddle shoes. "You look great," Tess said as she placed the navy brimmed cap on Mattie's head.

"Okay, you two, let's get going," Sebastian piped in, grabbing his suit coat from the back of the chair and putting it on.

The family walked the few blocks to Mattie's new school. Some children were already running around the concrete playground as they entered the fenced property. A young blonde woman, who seemed to be in her twenties, was trying to calm a crying child. They approached the teacher. Mattie walked up to the little boy and said, "Are you hurt?"

The boy sniffled and said, "My mum left me here. I want to go home."

"My name is Mattie Irons. What's your name?"

"My name is Michael Symonds."

Mattie extended her hand in greeting. Michael wiped a stray tear from his cheek with the back of his hand. Then he shook her hand.

"You must be Miss Abernathy," Sebastian said.

The teacher looked at Sebastian and Tess and gave them a warm smile. "Yes—nice to meet you Mr. and Mrs. Irons." She looked down at Mattie and Michael. "Michael, would you like to go play with Mattie on the swing set?"

Michael nodded in agreement, and soon he and Mattie where walking over to the swings and laughing.

"That's quite a young lady you have there," the teacher complimented.

"She has her father's charm," Tess agreed.

"Don't forget to take her picture," Sebastian reminded.

Tess reached for the Nikon in her handbag and they walked over to the swing set. "Mattie, Mummy wants to take a photo of your first day at school," Sebastian said, gaining her attention.

"Can Michael be in the photo, too?"

"Sure, come stand here for me," Tess instructed, pointing to a spot that was bathed in sunlight.

The children posed with a smile and Mattie took Michael's hand as Tess snapped the shot. "Charming—just like her father," Tess reiterated. "Just wait until she comes home and tells us she has a boyfriend."

"Over my dead body," Sebastian muttered, before kissing Tess on the temple.

They hugged Mattie goodbye and walked to the Tube station so they could each get to their separate destinations. "Love you. Have a good day," Tess said, giving him a quick kiss on the cheek.

"See you tonight."

Sebastian walked into Fiona Ashford Gallery in Kensington and greeted the manager, Duncan Kincaid, a rotund fellow with glasses and thinning hair. "Good morning."

"Hello, Sebastian. Did you get Mattie off to school this morning?"

"Yes, she's already making friends."

"Ah, I remember those days when the missus and I sent our children off to school. Now they are married with children of their own."

"Time flies," Sebastian agreed.

"Indeed, enjoy this time with her."

"Is the new acquisition from Hirst scheduled to arrive today?" Sebastian asked as he stood behind the counter and opened the email on the computer.

"No, Fiona scheduled it for Friday."

The sleek cordless phone rang and Duncan answered the call. "One moment, please." Duncan placed his hand over the receiver and said in a soft voice, "It's for you."

"Irons here."

"Sebastian, Mr. Minton wants to meet us as soon as possible. He's found Father," Maxwell announced.

Sebastian clutched the edge of the counter and took a deep breath, unable to speak.

"Sebastian, are you there?" Max asked with concern in his voice.

He moved his tongue around his dry mouth until he could finally speak. "Yes," he whispered.

"Can you get over to my office straightaway?"

"Yes."

"See you soon." Max rung off and Sebastian stood unmoving, unable to process what was happening.

"Are you all right? Can I fetch you some tea?" Duncan inquired.

Sebastian shook his head, refusing the beverage. "I'm sorry, Duncan. I have a family emergency. Do you mind if I leave?"

"Is your little one okay?" Duncan gravely asked.

"It's not Mattie. I must go."

"Of course. Good luck, Sebastian."

With that Sebastian was out the door, standing on the curb and hailing a black cab. His mind was reeling and he didn't trust himself to take the Tube, lest he miss his stop. The cabbie stopped and Sebastian got in the back seat of the cab. He gave the driver the address of his intended destination and they were on their way, weaving in and out London traffic, heading toward Westminster.

Mr. Minton was already seated in Maxwell's office when Sebastian arrived twenty minutes later. Too nervous to sit, he looked at Minton and waited for an explanation. "I was able to locate your father." The investigator paused a little too long for Sebastian's liking and then continued. "He's alive and living on the island of Corfu on the Ionian Sea."

"He's living in the Greek Islands," Max said, unbelieving.

Sebastian loosened his necktie and sat down next to Minton. "He's alive. How did you find him?"

"Several phone calls and personal interviews. It wasn't an easy task."

"Have you made contact with him specifically? Does he know we're looking for him?" Max asked.

"I've not made contact. As we agreed when we started this journey, once I found Mr. Baker, it would be up to you whether you chose to meet him or not." Minton opened his briefcase and pulled out identical reports. He handed one to Max and the other to

Sebastian. "Here is all the information you need. I believe my work here is completed."

Maxwell stood to shake the investigator's hand. "Well done, Minton. I'll have my secretary send over the final payment."

"Much appreciated, Mr. Irons."

With that, Mr. Minton closed his briefcase and was out the door. Sebastian remained silent, staring at the report in front of him that contained the location of his father's residence.

Maxwell walked over to the sideboard and poured a finger of scotch into a crystal tumbler. Handing it to his brother, he said, "You look like you could use this."

Sebastian glanced up at Max and gratefully took the glass, downing its contents in one gulp.

"For Christ's sake, say something, Sebastian."

He ran his fingers through his hair and sighed. "When he said the money was going into a Swiss bank account, I figured he'd never be able to trace it. I'm shocked."

"Are you pleased?" Maxwell pressed.

"Yes," he softly replied, lost in thought for a moment, and then said, "Will you come to Greece with me?"

Max said down next to Sebastian. "This is your journey, not mine. Father knew I existed and he left anyway. If getting yearly support from Mother was more important to him than keeping a relationship with his children, I want nothing to do with the man. I have a wedding to plan."

Sebastian couldn't argue with Maxwell's logic, because he would most likely feel the same way if the roles were reversed. "I have to talk to Tess."

"Absolutely. Go to her."

"Thanks, Max—for everything."

Filled with anxiety, Sebastian made his way to the Associated Press office. Tess was the only person who could talk him off the ledge he was standing on. The lift dinged as it reached her floor. Walking up to the receptionist's desk, he got a smile from the young woman when she recognized him. Before he could speak, she was on the phone paging Tess.

Tess came rushing toward him, her face bathed in confusion. "What is it? What's the matter?" she desperately questioned. "Is it Mattie?"

How could he be so daft to alarm her this way? "Mattie is fine." He handed Tess the report he was clutching in his hand. "Minton found my father."

Tess took Sebastian by the hand and walked him back to her cubicle so they could have some privacy. They sat down facing one another, Tess still holding his hand, not bothering to read the report. "He's alive then?"

Sebastian nodded affirmative. "Living on a small Greek island."

"That's good, right?" she slowly asked, her voice unsteady.

He bounced his right leg up and down with nervous energy. "I don't know," he whispered softly. "I feel so many things: confusion, frustration, hopeful yet discouraged. I'm utterly lost."

"Of course you feel all those things. I'd be worried if you didn't. This is a huge development." Tess squared her shoulders and looked Sebastian in the eyes. "We should go see him—together," she decided with great determination.

"I don't think I could do it without you, Tess."

"Then we'll fly to Greece. If you don't like what you find, we can turn around and come right back."

Sebastian lunged forward and wrapped his arms around his amazing wife, hugging her so desperately she almost couldn't breathe. "God, I love you."

"I love you, too," she said, pulling back just enough so she could kiss him. She glanced at the clock on her desk. "Mattie will be getting out of school soon. Let's go pick her up together."

"Can you leave?"

"I have an article I'm working on that I can finish at home. I'll clear it with the boss."

Sebastian kissed her hand and then closed his eyes and placed his cheek against her knuckles. "Thank you."

Tess left him momentarily to visit her boss in his corner office and discuss her plans. When she walked back into her cubicle ten minutes later, she grabbed her purse and Sebastian carried her briefcase, and they exited the building together. She reached for his hand and asked, "The wedding's in two weeks. Do you want to go to Greece before or after?"

"I don't know. Who will watch Mattie? Can you get some time off work that quickly?"

"I don't think I could wait if I were you."

"It's been twenty-five years."

"And you seem anxious. The sooner the better, I say."

"Rip the bandage off quickly, in other words," he added.

"Exactly. I know this whole situation has you in knots. I don't want to prolong it. The quicker we do this, the quicker you can stop wondering and move on." They walked down the stairs into the Tube station and navigated through the tunnels until they reached their platform. "Let me call my mom. Maybe she can schedule a visit and take care of Mattie while we go find your father."

"Let's do it. I'm not sure how much longer I can take not knowing the outcome of this impending meeting."

# Chapter 18 - What You Need

With haste, Sebastian and Tess made travel arrangements. A week later, they were picking Kate Hamilton up at Heathrow International Airport. Mattie jumped up and down as she spied Kate walking out of customs. "Grandmom!"

Kate gave the trio a wide smile. First, she picked Mattie up and hugged her. "How's my favorite granddaughter?"

"Great!" Mattie replied as Kate set her back down on the floor.

Next she hugged Tess. "It's so good to see you, honey. I've missed you all so much." Then she hugged Sebastian.

"How was your flight?" he inquired.

"Good. Thank you for picking me up."

Sebastian took Kate's suitcase and led the group to the car port. The sky was misty and gray—typical English weather. He didn't mind that the three girls chatted nonstop as he drove them back to London in the car he borrowed from Penny. The plan was to spend a few days with Kate to acclimate her to the city before he and Tess flew to Corfu. Luckily, Tess' boss was very accommodating in giving her time off. He even managed assign her an article while she was in Greece.

After a tour of their neighborhood and a walk through Regent's Park, everyone settled in for a home-cooked meal. Sitting around the table, they talked and laughed. Sebastian was very happy Kate could make the trip, and had no qualms about leaving Mattie in her care.

As the day came to a close, Sebastian suggested Tess and her mom spend some time together, while he volunteered to put Mattie to bed. He sat next to her, his back propped against the headboard reading her a bedtime story.

"Why aren't you doing the voices?" she asked.

"I'm sorry, Mattie. My mind's on other things."

"Will you miss me when you go to Greece?"

"Of course—but you are so lucky to have Grandmom Kate here to look after you."

"Can she take me to school tomorrow so she can meet Michael?"

"Just what's going on between you and Michael?" he asked in a stern tone of voice.

Mattie simply giggled. "Michael is my best friend, Daddy."

"You only just met the chap a week ago."

Mattie looked at her father and rolled her eyes.

"You are going to be a handful, aren't you?"

"What does that mean?"

"Oh, nothing," he wearily sighed.

"Daddy, you're weird."

"That's not a very nice thing to say, Martha," he scolded.

"I love you." She curled her small arms around his waist and laid her head on his stomach.

"Enough reading for tonight. Shall I stay here until you fall asleep?"

Mattie nodded her head and closed her eyes. Within ten minutes, she was fast asleep.

Tess and Kate sat on the couch, drinking wine and talking. "I'm so glad you love London," Kate admitted.

"It's been incredible, Mom. Mattie has transitioned so well. I love my job at the AP. Sebastian is getting to know his older brother and sister." She shook her head, pondering all the changes. "So much has happened in such a short amount of time."

"And soon he'll have the chance to meet his father."

"Yes, I pray it goes well. He won't admit it, but Sebastian needs him to be a good man. If he's not, I'm not sure how Bas will handle it."

"Don't worry. Stay positive."

Tess hugged her mom. It was so good to have her there. "I'm sorry you have to sleep on the sofa bed. You can have our bed when we go."

"Honey, I'd sleep on the floor for a chance to be with my family. Sebastian was very kind to offer to put me up in a hotel, but I did not fly seven thousand miles to be alone."

Sebastian walked into the room carrying fresh linens to make up the bed. "Mattie is asleep. I thought you might like to turn in, Kate."

"Thank you. I didn't get much sleep on the flight. I was so excited to see all of you."

Sebastian moved the coffee table and began to convert the couch into a bed. Tess helped him cover it with bed sheets. "Sleep well, Kate," Sebastian said, kissing his mother-in-law's cheek.

"I'm heading out early in the morning so I can leave the office at three o'clock to come home, have dinner with you, and pack," Tess added, hugging her mom again. "You and Bas can take Mattie to school."

"Goodnight."

Tess was out of the house and at the office by seven o'clock the next morning. Sebastian made eggs and toast for Mattie and Kate before they walked her to school. The sun was peeking through the clouds and it was shaping up to be a lovely day. While Mattie attended school, Sebastian was going to play tour guide and answer any questions Kate might have about her stay. After Mattie introduced Grandmom Kate to her teacher and her best friend, Michael, Sebastian and Kate were off to do some sightseeing.

They sat back in the red vinyl seats as the cruise boat sailed along the Thames River. They passed all the famous monuments that graced London's shoreline: Parliament, Big Ben, St. Paul's Cathedral, and Tower Bridge. "I'm grateful to you for making the trip so quickly, Kate. Everything is chaotic right now with Maxwell and Penny's wedding next weekend."

"Oh, I'm happy to do it. This has been the first vacation I've taken in…well, I don't remember. The hospital begged me to take the time off."

"I hope you'll come to the wedding."

"I don't even know your brother. I don't want to impose."

"Nonsense—the more the merrier. You already know Penny. Mattie is a flower girl and you'll get to see the castle," he explained, his lips creeping up into a smile.

"Well, how could I refuse!" Kate looked out the window, appreciating the view. "This is a wonderful city. I see why Tess loves it so much."

"Yes, she's happy here," he agreed.

Kate glanced over at Sebastian. "She's happy wherever she is as long as she's with you. I'm glad she's going with you to meet your father."

"I couldn't do it without her," he quietly admitted.

Kate placed a comforting hand on his shoulder. "I understand your reservations about meeting him. If you're meant to have a relationship with him, it will happen."

"And if it doesn't?"

"Then you must know that you are the most incredible and loving father I could ever wish for my granddaughter. You don't need to have a father to be a good one yourself."

Sebastian let out the breath he didn't even realize he'd been holding in. "Thank you, Kate."

"I know Lily was a terrible mother to you, and Nanny Jones was the closest thing to a mother you had in your life. I would be honored if you would call me Mom—or Mum, if that isn't English enough for you," she said with a wink.

"I would be happy to call you Mom."

They ate an early supper before heading off to the airport. Sebastian and Tess settled in for the three hour flight to Corfu. "How are you holding up?" Tess inquired.

"I feel good leaving Mattie in your Mom's care. I'm glad they'll get to spend some time together."

"That wasn't what I meant."

He turned and gave her a feeble smile. "I know."

Tess took his hand and squeezed it for support. "This will be over soon. For good or bad, you'll be able to put this past you and move on."

He didn't want to talk about his impending meeting with his father, so he changed the subject. "Your passport is getting quite the workout and we've only lived in London for three months."

"This is what I've dreamed about. All those years going to school and working hard—it's paid off. I feel like the luckiest girl in the world."

"I love seeing you so happy. You deserve every bit of success you receive."

"Mr. Irons, you are a big part of the reason I'm so successful," she acknowledged, leaning in and kissing him on the cheek.

"We make a great team, Mrs. Irons."

"Exactly—together we can do anything."

It was nine thirty in the evening by time they got to their hotel in Corfu City. It was a charming four-story sandstone building flanked by large palm trees at the entrance. The attendant held open the front door for the couple to enter. Sebastian guided Tess across the terra cotta tiled floor to the reception desk. After exchanging pleasantries with the concierge, they were given a room key and declined assistance with their carry-on bags.

The room, on the top floor of the hotel, was quiet and simply decorated with a queen-sized bed, an armchair next to the window, and a small desk. Their surroundings weren't opulent, but they were comfortable. "I like it. It's cozy," Tess said as she placed her bag on the luggage rack.

"We don't need anything fancy," Sebastian agreed. "We're not on holiday."

"Are you tired?" she asked, walking up behind him as he looked out the window.

"No—too keyed up," he admitted. There was no way he was going to be able to sleep when he was so close to seeing, maybe even meeting, his father.

"So what are we going to do about that?" Tess asked in a not-so-innocent tone of voice.

Sebastian turned away from the window to face his wife, who was slowly backing away from him as she undid the buttons of her gray silk blouse. A sexy grin etched across her lips as she reached the last button and slid the blouse off, placing it on the desk. He took a seat in the armchair to watch the show Tess was putting on for him. Next, she reached behind her waist and pulled down the zipper of her black skirt, shimmying the skirt over her hips until it pooled on the floor at her ankles. Stepping out of the skirt, she sauntered toward her husband in black lace lingerie Sebastian had never seen before. He sucked in a breath as he reveled in her beauty.

"I know the perfect way to get you mind off your troubles," she said in a low, seductive voice as she straddled his lap. Placing her fingers in his hair, she pulled him in for a kiss. It was deep and passionate, igniting a fire in his blood.

He moaned into her mouth, their tongues melding together, hot with need. His hands moved over the lace cups of her demi-bra and felt her nipples pebble under his touch. Sebastian's tongue licked the swell of exposed breast. Hooking a finger under the strap, he pulled it down and then moved to the other side. Soon her breasts were free and he eagerly latched onto the nipple with his mouth. Tess laced her fingers behind her head to give him better access, sighing with pleasure as he licked and sucked. Sliding his hands down her waist, he gripped the lace fabric of her panties. "Take these off, now," he ordered in a husky voice.

Tess stood up so she could comply with his demand. Meanwhile Sebastian frantically unbuckled his belt and lowered the zipper of his trousers to free his erection, holding his free hand out to Tess, who took it and positioned herself over the chair. Slowly she slid down onto his cock, grabbing onto his shoulders to steady herself.

Sebastian watched his gorgeous wife through heavy lidded eyes as she moved up and down with deliberate, artful strokes. His hands caressed her naked thighs, so soft and silky to the touch. "So fucking amazing," he muttered, his eyes clamped on hers.

"You do this to me, Bas. Only you can make me feel this way." She blushed before reclaiming his mouth. Tess picked up the pace and Sebastian flexed his hips to meet her demand. At this pace, he wouldn't last much longer, feeling the excitement build in his groin and start to spread through every nerve ending. With one last thrust, he pushed into her, up to the hilt, and exploded. "Oh, Tess, damn!"

She collapsed into his arm, leaning her forehead on his shoulder, panting for breath.

"We aren't finished yet, darling. Hold onto me." With that he stood from the chair, Tess' legs wrapped around his waist. He walked the short distance to the bed and laid her down on the mattress.

She was naked except for the silk thigh-high stockings and leather pumps she had left on. Sebastian shrugged out of his suit coat, followed by this white shirt, and then his trousers. Kneeling down on the floor in front of his wife, he removed her shoes. Next he carefully rolled down the stockings, planting light kisses along her leg as he went. Once she was completely naked, he leaned back on his calves and gave her a devilishly wicked grin. Placing his hands on Tess' thighs, he spread them open and then leaned forward to touch her, his fingers sliding up and down against her sex. She was so wet and ready for him, and now he was going to make her come. Slipping a finger inside her, he licked his lips before placing his tongue on her swollen clit.

Tess arched her back to meet his advances. The onslaught of his tongue and fingers worked her into a frenzy. Leaning up on her elbows, she looked down to see Sebastian peering up to glance at her, his eyes alight with mischief. "My cheeky Bas," she panted between ragged breaths. A few more expert flicks of his tongue sent her crashing over the edge in ecstasy.

Sebastian lay down next to Tess, instinctively pulling her into his arms. "I love how you distract me," he said before kissing her beautiful lips. "You wear me out."

"That's the idea," she giggled. "Let's get under the covers. I'm tired, too."

Reluctantly, Sebastian stood from the bed. He picked up his rumpled suit and Tess' lingerie and draped them over the armchair. Switching the light off, he crawled back into bed with his wife and cradled her in his arms. Within a few minutes, they both fell off to sleep.

# Chapter 19 - Oh, Father

Sebastian looked down at the paper in his hand that contained his father's address, and then he looked at the villa in front of him. It was a small one-story home with turquoise shutters and quaint flower boxes hanging from the windows. Now all he had to do was will his feet to move forward and knock on the wooden door. He glanced at Tess, who silently nodded her approval, and then took her hand. Together they walked to the entrance. Taking a deep breath, Sebastian raised his knuckles and rapped on the door.

After a few moments, the door opened. An older, slender woman—maybe in her fifties—with long raven hair greeted them. "Hello, how may I help you?" she asked in a French accent.

Sebastian wanted to answer her question, but his mouth was dry. He swallowed, trying to find his voice. Just then, a gentleman came up behind the woman, asking, "Colette, darling, do we have visitors?"

Sebastian stared at Martin Christopher Baker. The resemblance was alarming. It was as if Sebastian was looking at his reflection in the mirror and seeing himself age thirty-five years. His father's eyes were still bright blue, with soft wrinkle lines around them. Martin's hair was thick with a smattering of gray. His demeanor was happy and relaxed.

The couples stood on opposite sides of the doorframe staring at each other. Finally Sebastian said, "I'm Sebastian Irons and this is my wife, Tess. I'm your son."

Martin's mouth opened, surprised at the revelation. Colette looked up at Martin and then back to Sebastian. "Please come inside," she said, stepping aside to allow them entrance.

Once inside the home, the four of them stood in awkward silence. "I'm sorry to come unannounced," Sebastian apologized. "I realize this must come as quite a shock."

"Let's sit on the terrace. I'll get us some drinks," Colette suggested.

They followed the elegant French woman to the tiled terrace overlooking the Ionian Sea. "It's beautiful," Tess remarked, taking in the view.

Martin took a seat and ran his fingers through his hair. "Forgive my surprise. I'm usually not this quiet."

Colette let out a full, melodic laugh. "That is an understatement, mon cheri."

"When were you born?" Martin asked.

"May 27, 1967."

"Lily was pregnant when we divorced?"

"Yes."

"If I had known…"

"What—what would you have done? Given up the payments she's been making to you for years?" Sebastian asked with disgust.

"How did you find me?" Martin demanded to know.

"It wasn't easy, believe me," Sebastian spat.

"Okay, let's just take a moment and breathe," Tess suggested, breaking up the brewing fight.

"Tess, this was a big mistake. We should go."

"Sebastian, I didn't know you existed," Martin began, his voice softer and calmer. "Please don't go."

Colette walked out onto the terrace carrying a tray of beverages. She passed out the drinks and joined the others at the oblong wrought-iron table. "Martin, I can't get over how much he looks like you when you were younger."

"Have you and Martin been together for a long time?" Tess asked.

"Oh, yes. It's been twenty years now. We met in Monte Carlo." She threw her head back, looking up at the sky, and reminisced. "Do you remember that day, Martin?"

Martin reached over and caressed her hand. "I remember it like it was just yesterday. But I must say you look far more lovely today."

Sebastian grimaced. Martin reminded him too much of himself, and that knowledge didn't bring him any comfort. "You've been married for twenty years?"

"We're not married," Martin informed the young couple.

"We're living in sin and it's delightful!" Colette chimed in.

"You've been monogamous for twenty years?" Sebastian rephrased.

"Yes, why do you ask?"

Sebastian shrugged. "Wasn't that the reason Lily divorced you in the first place?"

"Your mother wasn't the easiest person to live with."

"I'm more than aware of that fact."

"Have you had a good life, Sebastian?"

"That's an odd question considering you left my brother and sisters without a second thought."

Martin sighed. "I loved those children the best way I knew how."

"Loved—that's past tense. Did you feel any remorse at all leaving them?"

"Of course I did. My hands were tied. Your mother comes from a very powerful family. I could either leave with a handsome stipend or leave a penniless fool. Either way, I was banned from ever seeing my children again. What would you have done if you were in my circumstance?"

Sebastian chuckled at the irony of the entire situation. "I gave up the money and walked away."

"You are a better man than I am." Martin closed his eyes, becoming introspective. "How are they: Maxwell, Victoria, and Sigourney?"

"They are well," Sebastian replied, not going into detail.

"Do you still have contact with your mother?"

"Lily's not my mother."

Martin stared at Sebastian, a look of confusion in his eyes. "Who was your mother, then?"

Given his father's philandering, that probably wasn't the best way to word the statement. "Lily is my biological mother, but she was *never* a mother to me."

"I'm so sorry, my boy," Martin stated with sincerity.

"I'm not *your* boy," Sebastian ground out with contempt.

"I sense you didn't have the best childhood."

"My childhood was fine. It was my teenage years that proved to be difficult."

"What do you mean by that?"

"Nothing," Sebastian replied, brushing the question aside.

"Why are you here today?"

"I wanted to meet my birth father. I wanted to see if you had any remorse for leaving us."

Tess reached over and squeezed his knee with her hand. Instinctively, his hand closed around hers.

"I made my decision and I've had to live with that. I don't believe in remorse. Maybe when you get older, you'll understand."

Sebastian threw his fist down on the table, rattling the glasses that rested on top. "I understand the ramifications of hard decisions. I also know the difference between doing what is right and wrong. You have no right to pass judgment on me when you don't even know me."

"I could say the same of you," Martin coolly added.

Sebastian stood from his chair so quickly it toppled over, making a clanking sound as it hit the patio. "We're through here, Tess."

She stood and Sebastian led her into the house and out the front door.

They walked a few blocks before he decided to speak. "That daft prick!" he fumed, gripping her hand even harder than before.

"I'm sorry it didn't turn out the way you wanted," Tess finally said.

"I'm not sure I fucking know what I expected. It was stupid of me to come here and drag you along."

"To hell with Martin. You don't need him." Tess leaned into her husband and wrapped her arm around his waist. "I'm not sorry you dragged me along. We did have a wonderful night last night."

His expression softened has he recalled their lovemaking. "It was wonderful. Are you trying to distract me again?"

"Maybe," she replied, giving him a coy smile.

"You know what? Martin doesn't deserve to take up another moment of my thought." He reached for his wife's hand, deciding to leave all the misery behind him and focus on the positive. Life was too short to spend it lamenting over Martin Christopher Baker. "Let's enjoy the day. We can consider it a mini-vacation before we have to go back to the hoopla that will be Max and Penny's wedding. By the way, I invited your mom to the wedding. I figured one more person to look after Mattie isn't a bad thing, and maybe I can enjoy a few dances alone with you."

They walked down to the beach, each taking off their shoes before stepping onto the soft sand. "Do you think Lily will skip the service, like she did the engagement party?"

"I imagine so, although it would look bad from a social standpoint to do so. You know how she feels about propriety."

"Well, I hope she stays away for everyone's sake," Tess sighed. "Things are so much easier without all the drama."

They stopped walking and sat down, looking over the clear green Ionian Sea. "Why is it that my family comes with all the drama and your family is so laid back?"

"Well, considering it's only my mom and me—how much drama could there be? Not to mention the fact that there is something to be said for living a simpler life."

Tess certainly had a point. He loved the life he lived with his family, not regretting for one moment the aristocracy he'd left behind. The only problem was that now he was being dragged back into it. "Maybe getting close to my brother and sister again is a bad idea."

"Why would you say that?"

"I'm getting pulled back into that world and dragging you and Mattie along with me."

"Bas, I like your brother and sisters. If you want a relationship with them, you should have it. That decision has nothing to do with Lily or your father. You're lucky you have siblings. I always wanted them. Now I sort of feel like I do, the way they welcomed me into the family."

"That's sweet of you to say, but you're being way too kind."

"I don't think I am. They accept me for who I am—something Lily never did. They also adore Mattie. What more could I ask?"

Again, his wife had taken the complicated and reduced it to something so basic and simple. "You are the most brilliant person I know," he complimented, leaning down to kiss the top of her head.

"I have my moments," she grinned. "Buy me lunch. I saw a cute little café down the street."

Sebastian stood and patted the sand off his trousers. He extended his hand to Tess and pulled her into an upright position. "For you—anything," he replied pulling her into his arms and kissing her on the lips.

# Chapter 20 - The Disappointed

Tess walked through the door first, followed by Sebastian, who carried their luggage. Mattie ran at them full force and jumped into Tess' open arms. "Welcome home!"

Sebastian placed the bags on the floor and scooped Mattie up in his arms. "How's my favorite girl?"

"Awesome!"

"Did you have a nice time with Grandmom Kate?"

"Yep."

Tess hugged her mom. "Hope she behaved for you."

"We had an amazing time. How did things go in Greece?" Kate inquired.

Tess shook her head. "Later," she replied.

"Did you bring me anything, Daddy?"

Sebastian raised his eyebrows. "What makes you think that?"

Mattie giggled. "Daddy, you always bring me something when you go away on a trip."

"I'll make you a deal: you go get your pajamas on and I'll look through my suitcase and see what I can find."

"Yay!" she exclaimed, racing down the hall to her room.

Kate hugged Sebastian. "I'm sorry things didn't go like you wanted them to."

"I have no regrets. I've spent years wondering about him and now I know. Deep down, I never expected a happy ending on that front."

"Would you like some tea? I can put the kettle on." Kate offered.

"Yes, I'd like that." Sebastian picked up the bags. "Let me go get Mattie's present before she gets all riled up and I can't get her to bed."

"I'll come with you," Tess offered.

"No, I've got it. Stay here and fill your mom in on the trip."

"Is he really okay?" Kate asked as she busied herself in the kitchen.

"Yes, we had a good talk. I think he's reconciled with the fact that Martin won't be a part of his life. I mean, he never was to start with, so it's not like he's losing a father—not like me," she said, full of melancholy. They sat down at the kitchen table together. "Bas told me you're going to the wedding. I'm so happy you'll be there."

"I can't wait to see this castle you've told me so much about."

"It's pretty spectacular and intimidating."

"We'll need to go shopping. I don't have a dress."

"Mattie and I can take you shopping. I'm so glad you're here, Mom. I've missed you. I don't suppose you'd quit your job and move to London, would you?"

"Don't tempt me."

"I'm serious. You could sell the house and move. You can work at a hospital here in London."

"Where would I live?"

"We could help you find a place," Tess offered.

The tea kettle whistled, taking their attention away from the conversation at hand. Kate walked over the stove and turned off the burner. Tess plopped the tea bags into the mugs while her mom poured the hot water. Finally Kate said, "It's not a bad idea, you know. I'll give it some careful consideration."

Sebastian tucked Mattie under the covers and then placed a teddy bear on each side of her—Charles on the left and Bas on the right. "Love you, darling," he said, kissing her forehead.

"I'm glad you're back, Daddy."

"So am I."

With that he turned out the lights and left her bedroom, closing the door behind him. It was such an amazing feeling to have this little person who loved him unconditionally and be genuinely happy to see him.

As he walked toward his bedroom, Sebastian wondered if Martin Christopher Baker ever felt a pang of regret for leaving his children behind. With a weary hand, he unknotted his tie and then took off his suit coat. Sebastian tossed the discarded clothes on the bed in his room and sat on the mattress. He grabbed the phone and dialed Max's number.

After a few brief rings, Max answered the phone. "Irons here."

"Max, it's Sebastian."

"I take it from your tone of voice things didn't go as anticipated."

"They went exactly as I anticipated. He didn't give a damn."

"I'm sorry, Sebastian. I tried to warn you."

"I know." He paused for a moment and then said, "How does a father not care what happens to his children, Max?"

"I wish I knew. I'm not a father yet, but when it does happen for me, I hope I can be as good a father as you are," Max responded.

Sebastian smiled. "Thank you. That is a lovely compliment."

"It's the truth."

"How are the wedding plans coming along?"

"Penelope is in charge. I just pay the bills," Max chuckled.

"Any word from Lily?"

"I told her she could come or stay away. I really don't care what her opinion is. The person I marry is my choice. She has no say in the decision. If she does come, Penelope will be sure to keep you separated. You won't have to converse with her."

"I don't plan to, you can be sure of that."

"I'll see you next weekend."

"Give Pen my love. Goodnight, Maxwell."

Sebastian joined Tess and Kate a short while later. "Everything okay?" Tess asked.

"Yes. She loved her necklace and is wearing it to bed."

"We found a sterling silver necklace with a Pegasus horse charm on it in one of the markets," Tess explained.

"She's quite taken with horses. I got to hear all about how Sebastian is teaching her to ride and Uncle Max bought her a riding outfit," Kate said.

"We've come a long way from Spring City, Pennsylvania, Mom."

"Well, *you* have, Tess. I don't know about me."

"So are you ladies going shopping tomorrow?"

"Yes, after work. Mom, can you and Mattie meet me at Selfridges?"

"I don't know where that is."

"I'll take you," offered Sebastian. "I'm only working half the day tomorrow and there are some things I need to do on Bond Street. Maybe we can all have dinner afterwards."

"That sounds great."

"Okay, I'll make reservations."

# Chapter 21 - White Wedding

The castle was bristling with excitement as the staff prepared for Maxwell and Penelope's wedding. Many of the guests had arrived the night before, including Sebastian and his family.

Tess tied the blue satin bow at the back on Mattie's flower girl dress. It was an ivory silk calf-length dress, with short sleeves and a Peter Pan collar. She wore knee socks and black patent leather shoes and a wreath of rosebuds and baby's breath on her head. "You look so pretty, Mattie."

"Let me see," she said, rushing toward the full-length mirror.

Sebastian knocked on the door. "Are you ladies ready?" he asked, poking his head inside.

"Daddy, do you like my dress?"

Sebastian walked into the room and admired his daughter. "Darling, you look wonderful. You're growing up too fast."

"I wish Michael could be here." She frowned.

"You're growing up too fast," Sebastian reiterated.

Mattie smirked and rolled her eyes.

"I brought you the flower basket."

"Spread the flowers just like you did in rehearsal yesterday," Tess reminded her daughter.

"Okay. Can I go see Grandmom Kate now?"

"Yes, she should be dressed," Tess agreed.

Mattie tore out of the room to find her grandmother. Sebastian chuckled. "You might think she runs the castle, the way she makes herself at home."

Tess looked at Sebastian. "She doesn't know the history of this place. Some things are better left alone."

Tess was wearing her pale pink Chanel gown with her hair pulled up in a loose bun. She approached her husband and smiled. "You look very dapper in your tuxedo."

"You look incredible, as always," he complimented, taking her in his arms. "I want to kiss you but I fear I won't be able to stop—and we have a wedding to attend."

Tess let out a languid sigh. "You're right. Best we go get Mattie and Mom.

Sebastian took her hand and raised it to his lips and kissed it. "I swear you look more beautiful today than you did on our wedding day."

Tess blushed at the compliment. "And you are far more charming."

They walked down the hallway toward Kate's room. The door was wide open and Mattie was entertaining Kate with stories about riding horses on the grounds. "Mattie, come with me, we need to get you downstairs. Aunt Penny needs you," Sebastian reminded her.

Mattie hopped off the bed and took Sebastian's hand and they left the room.

"This place…" Kate began, and then stopped, unsure what to say next.

"Pretty overwhelming—I know," Tess finished.

"I can't imagine what it must have been like for Sebastian, having to grow up here."

"He had some happy times when he was younger—with Nanny Jones."

"Do you think Lily will be here today?"

"I don't think so. She wasn't very happy with Max's choice of a wife."

"How sad for the Irons children to grow up without supportive parents," Kate said.

"All things considered, they're remarkably normal—well, as normal as wealthy people can be." Tess giggled to lighten the mood. "Come on, let's go see how an earl throws a wedding." Tess linked her arm in her mom's and together they walked down the grand staircase and out to the back garden.

White chairs with blue velvet seat cushions were neatly arranged in rows. There must have been two hundred chairs by Tess' estimation. A long white cloth runner was used to make an aisle that led to an ancient stone gazebo decorated with leafy green garland and pink peonies. The sky was clear blue with wisps of thin clouds. It was a perfect day for an outdoor wedding.

Sebastian found the two women admiring the transformation of the garden. He took Tess' arm and escorted her down the aisle. Kate followed close behind with her escort. Sebastian sat between his wife and his mother-in-law as the remainder of the guests filed in to their seats.

Ten minutes later, the orchestra began to play "Overture" by George Frederic Handel. Mattie began the slow procession down the aisle, sprinkling pink rose petals on the ground as she made her way toward the gazebo. Sigourney followed next, wearing a blue chiffon strapless gown, her hair long and perfectly in place. She carried a nosegay of peonies. After she had taken her place at the front, everyone stood to greet the bride.

Penelope was breathtaking. She wore a strapless white dress with a fitted ruched bodice and a long skirt with a tulle overlay. Her hair was pulled up to show off her long, slender neck and the diamond and sapphire necklace Maxwell had given her as a wedding gift. A short silk veil was attached to her head with his grandmother's Cartier diamond diadem. She carried a bouquet of peonies and white roses. Penny walked down the aisle, self-assured and beaming with happiness.

Maxwell waited at the end of the aisle for his bride to arrive. He was so riveted with her beauty, he couldn't take his eyes off her. She was elegant, poised, warm, and loving—everything he could ever want in a mate.

When she arrived next to Maxwell, she handed her bouquet to Sigourney. The bridesmaids and groomsmen took their seats in the front row and the minister began the ceremony. Sebastian held Tess' hand as the officiant talked about love, respect, and friendship. He was so happy for his brother and best friend. Even though he had been skeptical of their relationship at first, he had come to realize they truly loved one another. After all, love knows no timelines, and the speed at which one person could capture the heart of another could not be metered. They really were a perfect match, just like Tess and he were perfect together. The couple recited their vows, opting to go the traditional route and exchange platinum wedding bands. Twenty minutes later, the couple were pronounced husband and wife.

The crowd politely applauded as the couple made their way down the aisle to form a receiving line. As people passed by offering their congratulations and best wishes, Penny and Max smiled, happy and in love.

The guests adjourned in the ballroom for dinner. The room was transformed by round tables, flower arrangements, garlands, and candles. Sebastian had never seen the room so alive and festive—not even at Christmastime when he was a child.

The tables were dressed in ivory linen, fine Royal Dalton china, and Arthur Price silver. An elegant floral arrangement sat at the center of each table, while calligraphy place cards announced each guest's seat.

"This is spectacular. Even in my wildest dreams I couldn't have imagined how beautiful and extravagant this day would be," Kate announced as they took their seats at the table.

"This is understated. If Mother were in charge, it would truly be over the top," Victoria explained.

"Yes, well, thank God she's not here and Max had to good sense to marry Penny even when she disapproved," Sebastian said.

"Penny's from a perfectly respectable family," Victoria agreed. "I can't understand why Mummy wouldn't approve."

Kate leaned in and whispered to Tess, "So this is how the other half lives."

Tess nodded her head. "It takes some getting used to."

The uniformed waiters began dinner service. Everything was perfect and timed to the minute. "Mattie's so well behaved," Kate said, astonished.

"I know she can be a ball of energy, but she's taken to this lifestyle like a fish to water. I guess it's in her blood."

"She's young—it's easy for children to adapt."

"She better not get too used to it. Bas and I can't afford to buy a castle—let alone hire a staff to run it," Tess laughed.

"It's a good thing Max and Penny adore her. It takes the heat off of you and Sebastian."

"Just what do you two have your heads together about over here?" Sebastian leaned in and whispered.

"Your daughter's good manners and ease of living in all this opulence," Kate replied.

"She's amazing, isn't she?"

After dinner was consumed, dancing began. "Ladies and gentleman, may I introduce the Earl and Countess of Sutton," the liveried butler announced as Max and Penny took the floor for their first dance. The orchestra began to play "The Best Is Yet To Come." Max took Penny in his arms and together they moved with elegant grace on the dance floor like Fred Astaire and Ginger Rogers.

As the evening wore on, copious amounts of champagne were consumed, toasts were made, and the lavish six-tiered wedding cake was cut and served. The party began to slow down around eleven o'clock. Sebastian and Tess were some of the last guests to retire for the evening.

"What a lovely day," Tess said, sitting down to remove her shoes back in the comfort of their guest room.

"It was, wasn't it?" Sebastian agreed as he took off his jacket and loosened his bow tie.

"I feel a little tipsy," she admitted. "Will you unzip me?"

"Is that all you want?" he asked in a low, seductive tone. He kissed her neck and slowly pulled the zipper down to reveal her soft skin.

"I think I can be persuaded to have a little fun."

"A *little* fun," Sebastian teased.

Tess giggled. "There's nothing *little* about it."

"That's better," he agreed, slipping the dress off his wife.

As they lay in bed after making love, Tess traced the plane of Sebastian's bare chest with her fingers. "Gosh, it's been a whirlwind couple of weeks. I feel like I need a vacation to recuperate from everything."

"I feel the same way," he agreed, gently stroking Tess' long brown hair. "I have an idea: let's go away for Christmas—back to New Jersey. No castle or fancy parties, just the three of us, your mom, and Henry and Alice."

"I like the idea. I miss Henry and Alice," Tess said. "Doesn't it seem like we're always on the go? I don't think we were ever this busy back in New York."

"I think you're right," Sebastian conceded. "I miss Henry and Alice, too."

"Maybe things will fall into a nice calm pattern now that we found your father and the wedding is over."

"We can only hope."

# Chapter 22 - Not Enough Time

It was a crisp, cool, Saturday morning in November. Sebastian pulled Penny's car up to the front door of the castle and turned off the ignition. Mattie was already unbuckling her seat belt and opening the back door. Max and Penny walked down the stone steps to greet them. It was a bank holiday weekend, so Sebastian took his family out to the country to visit the newlyweds.

"Uncle Max!" Mattie bellowed, running up the steps toward her uncle.

Max scooped her up in his arms and gave her a hug. "Hello, Mattie!"

"Did you have a nice honeymoon?"

"Yes, it was marvelous."

"Do you have any pictures?"

"Martha, we just got here," Sebastian chided. "Take a breath. Give Uncle Max some space."

"Come inside, we'll have some tea," Penny said, ushering everyone into the house while the servants unloaded the bags from the car.

Mattie took the lead, followed closely by Sebastian and Maxwell, while Penny and Tess lagged behind. "You are glowing," Tess complimented. "Did you have a wonderful time?"

Penny took Tess' hand and gave a broad smile. "It was magical. I so hope I'm pregnant. I can't wait to have little ones running about the place."

"Mattie would love that."

"Don't you and Sebastian ever think about having another child?"

"Maybe in a few years. There's still a lot I have to accomplish in my career before I go thinking about it."

"But you're so good with Mattie,"

Tess chuckled. If Penny only knew the struggles with depression she'd encountered throughout the pregnancy and after Mattie's birth. Tess didn't always feel like the perfect mother—in fact, she thought she was adequate, but that was all. It was the one thing she wasn't perfect at, and it always nagged at her. Fortunately, Sebastian made up for her shortcomings in the parenting department. "Sebastian gets all the credit. Everything I've learned has been from him."

Victoria and Sigourney joined them for dinner in the formal dining room later that evening. "I don't understand how Max manages to keep Lily away, but I'm grateful," Sebastian muttered to Sigourney, who sat next to him.

"That's easy," Sigourney responded, sipping her wine. "He's given her the Mayfair house and tells her when he'll be here so she doesn't show up unexpectedly. It's something similar to a shared visitation arrangement."

"And she's fine with this?"

"I doubt it, but she doesn't speak of it."

"So Max and Penny stay at her townhouse in Kensington when they're in London?"

"Yes, it works out nicely for all parties involved," Sigourney replied. "Honestly, I don't understand why everyone can't get along."

"She kicked me out of the family. Maxwell invited her to the wedding and she choose not to attend. If you ask me, she's the one with the problem."

"She is stubborn, I'll grant you that."

"I've had enough drama to last me a lifetime. I'm better off without her in my life."

"Sad but true."

Max spoke up from the other end of the table. "I thought we could all go fox hunting tomorrow. What do you say?"

"I want to go!" Mattie said, squirming in her seat with excitement.

"Martha, you aren't big enough to hunt yet. How many times to I need to explain this to you?" Sebastian questioned.

She turned her head to pout at her father and then looked at Tess. "Mummy?"

"Mattie, you are still learning to ride the pony. How about you and I go out for a ride tomorrow morning instead?"

The child shrugged her shoulders, resigned to her fate.

"When you are a little older and taller, I promise to teach you how to hunt," Max chimed in to cheer up the little girl.

After dinner, everyone retired to the drawing room for drinks and a game of cards. It wasn't bridge they played, however; somehow, Mattie conned everyone into a game of Go Fish. Sebastian sat back with Tess and watched as his brother and sisters played with his daughter.

"Of all the twist and turns that life could take, who would have thunk we'd end up here?" he said to Tess.

"With Mattie teaching a group of aristocrats how to play cards?"

"Exactly."

"Our baby girl is pretty spectacular," Tess agreed. "I know the first couple of years were bumpy. I could certainly have handled it better. We're so blessed we have her, Bas."

Sebastian kissed the top of her head. "I love you."

"Okay," she grinned, leaning her head against his shoulder.

The next day, the group was dressed in their riding attire and took off for a morning of sport. Tess and Mattie stayed behind for a leisurely ride around the grounds. The fog was just lifting off the dewy, verdant land as the hunting dogs raced forward and the riders followed behind at a gallop.

Sebastian enjoyed pushing the horse to its limits, jumping fences and feeling the sinewy muscles of the animal move under him. The fast pace of the horse and the adrenaline coursing through his veins warded off the chill in the air. He was racing alongside Maxwell, who gave him a sideways glance and grinned before kicking his horse to proceed faster, inching ahead of Sebastian.

Laughing, Sebastian wasn't about to give up the challenge and forged ahead in an attempt to beat Max, leaving his sisters far behind. As the animal gained speed and he was catching up to his brother, Max's horse reared tall with a loud whinny. Max was thrown backwards off the horse, who dropped to the ground next to Max. The horse writhed in pain.

Sebastian pulled on the reins hard to stop his horse. He jumped off the saddle and ran toward his fallen brother. "Max!" he yelled, falling to his knees and touching Max's chest. Maxwell's neck was twisted in an unnatural position, his blue eyes open wide, staring at Sebastian.

It was in that moment that he heard Penny scream. "No!"

Sebastian checked his wrist for a pulse and placed his hand in front of Max's mouth for any signs of breathing. Nothing. "Fuck! Max, don't do this!" he shouted.

When Penny reached them, she dropped to her knees and took Max's hand, staring at him in shock. Sigourney and Victoria rode in on their horses.

"Get an ambulance," Sebastian instructed.

His sisters took off without a word, racing back to the house for help.

It took an interminable twenty minutes for the medic to arrive. During that time Penny remained still, on her knees and holding Max's hand. There were no words spoken, no tears, just a shocked silence between Sebastian and Penny.

The stable hands had come to look at the horse. "Snake bite," one said aloud. "Let's get him back to the stable."

Maxwell wasn't that lucky: his neck had snapped in the fall, killing him instantly. It was certainly no comfort to any of his family. Sebastian pulled Penny away from her husband so the medics could do their work. They solemnly lifted Maxwell's body off the ground and placed him on a stretcher. Penny buried her head in Sebastian's chest to hide from the gruesome sight of her dead husband being driven away in an ambulance. Sebastian held onto her for dear life, as much for her sake as for his.

"Let's go back to the house," he gently urged.

"I'm not getting back on that horse," Penny whispered.

"We'll ride back with the stable hand," he said, guiding her to the waiting truck.

Sebastian was relieved that Tess and Mattie were nowhere in sight when the truck pulled up to the back entrance of the castle. He didn't want them to witness any of this. Penny clung to Sebastian as he walked her into the castle. Sigourney and Victoria were already back and had tea waiting in the sitting room. His sisters walked over to Penny, "Sit down, have some tea," Victoria instructed.

"I don't want any tea," she muttered.

Sebastian walked over to the sideboard and poured two glasses of scotch. He handed one to Penny and kept the other for himself. They glanced at each other, feeling sad and deflated, and swallowed the scotch in one gulp together.

"We should call Mother," Sigourney said to her siblings.

"You should do it," Victoria agreed.

Sigourney nodded and quietly left the room.

Sebastian noticed Tess and Mattie standing in the doorway. Tess was holding Mattie back by the shoulder, a sad and confused look on her face. Penny looked up, too; then she burst into tears. Sebastian shook his head, a nonverbal plea for Tess to leave the room and take Mattie with her.

"Mummy, what's wrong with Aunt Penny?" they heard her ask as Tess ushered her down the hallway.

Victoria handed Penny a tissue. Penny leaned her elbows on her thighs and placed her sobbing head in the palms of her hands. Victoria looked at Sebastian, unsure what to do next.

"Go find Sigourney. Give us some time alone," he said.

Victoria agreed, and with that she walked out of the room and closed the heavy double doors behind her.

Tess and Mattie were sitting on the staircase, their expressions full of worry. Victoria walked over to them. "What's happening?" Tess needed to know.

"Where's Uncle Max?" Mattie repeated.

"I think Mattie should go back to the nursery. We need to talk."

"I don't like the sound of this, Victoria."

"Please?"

"Mattie, please go to your room. Why don't you read a book while I find out what's happening, and I promise as soon as I know something, I'll come upstairs and fill you in."

"Okay, Mummy." Mattie whispered, and slowly climbed the stairs to her room.

"You said Max fell off his horse when you came up to call the ambulance. Why didn't Penny go with them to the hospital?"

Victoria winced at Tess' question. The reaction provided the answer to her inquiry.

Tess closed her eyes and took a deep breath. "No, not now. How could this have happened?"

"The horse suffered a snake bite and reared. Max was thrown from the horse. He snapped his neck," Victoria explained in a short burst of sentences.

Sigourney joined the two women. "Mother's been notified. She's getting the next flight out of Paris. She insists on making the funeral arrangements."

"Shouldn't that be Penny's job?" Tess asked.

"I don't know that she's in any frame of mind to do that right now," Victoria conceded.

"We should go see how she's doing," Sigourney said.

"No, Sebastian wanted some time alone with her. Leave them be for now."

~ ~ ~ ~

Penny was sobbing so hard, her entire body shook under Sebastian's protective hold on her. He tried rubbing her back in slow circles to calm her. Either it was beginning to work or she was just running out of tears. A dozen wet tissues were scattered on the floor at her feet.

Penny took a deep breath and slowly blew it out, trying to regulate her breathing. Finally she said, "What do I do now?"

It was a very big question and Sebastian wasn't sure how to respond. He took another tissue and gently dabbed the running mascara from her eyes, stalling to find the right words to comfort her.

Then she said, "What if I'm pregnant, Sebastian?"

"Then you'll always have a piece of Maxwell here with you."

"How can I raise a child alone?" she asked, her eyes brimming with tears once again.

"You aren't alone. Tess and I will help you. If he can't have his biological father, he can have me."

The tears spilled over again. "It's not fair. Why did this have to happen? Why now?"

"I don't know, Pen," he helplessly replied. "Do you want me to call the doctor? Maybe he can prescribe a sedative."

Penny nodded in agreement. "Anything to not think. I want to sleep."

The double doors partially opened and Sigourney popped her head into the room. Sebastian motioned for his sister to come forward. "Let me go call the doctor. Are you okay to stay here with Sigourney?"

Penny nodded again. Sebastian stood from the couch and pulled his sister aside.

In a hushed tone, she said, "I've informed Mother. She's on her way."

Resigned to the fact that he would have to face the woman he hated yet again, he shrugged his shoulders. "It's just as well. Penny is in no shape to handle funeral arrangements right now. Will you stay with her?"

"Of course."

Sebastian left the room to find Victoria and Tess talking by the stairs. They looked to him for answers that he didn't have. "Where's Mattie?" he asked them instead.

"In the nursery. I promised I'd go talk to her when I had information," Tess replied.

In the whirlwind of emotions, he'd forgotten he'd have to explain this all to Mattie. Crestfallen, he looked at Victoria. "Can you ring the doctor for Penny? She wants Valium."

Victoria agreed and left the couple alone. With that, Sebastian pulled his wife into his arms and kissed her for all he was worth. "Are you okay?" Tess asked, caressing the side of his face.

"No. All I keep thinking is 'thank God it wasn't me.'"

"I keep thinking the same thing, Bas. We'd be lost without you."

"This is so fucked up. They just got married. This wasn't supposed to happen."

"It doesn't seem real," Tess admitted. "Should we tell Mattie?"

"Let's go hold our girl and give her the bad news," Sebastian agreed.

They held hands as they ascended the marble staircase and made their way to Mattie's room.

# Chapter 23 - The Earl of Sutton

Inside the nursery, Mattie was sitting cross-legged looking through a picture book. She smiled when her parents entered the room.

"Mummy, can you tell me now?"

Tess sat on the bed to the right of Mattie. Sebastian sat on her left and pulled her onto his lap. "Uncle Max had an accident today," Sebastian began.

"Is he okay?"

"No, he was hurt very badly and he died," Tess responded.

Mattie looked up at Sebastian and then looked at Tess. "But I had breakfast with him this morning," Mattie stated in confusion.

"He fell off his horse when we were hunting, Mattie. It was a terrible accident. Sometimes bad things happen to good people," Sebastian further explained.

"What happens when you die?"

"You go to heaven to be reunited with all the people you love who died before you," Tess explained.

"So I'll get to see Uncle Max again someday?"

Sebastian chuckled. It was all he could do, astonished by the way his little girl was handling the situation. "Yes, you get to see him again, but not for a very long time."

"Daddy, promise me you won't go hunting again. I don't want you to die," Mattie said, wrapping her arms around his waist.

Tess rubbed a tear away with the back of her hand and glanced at Sebastian.

"I won't go hunting ever again. I promise."

"Where will Aunt Penny live without Uncle Max?"

"I suppose she'll stay at her house in Kensington."

"Then we have to visit her a lot so she's not lonely, Daddy."

"I agree."

Tess pushed a stray strand of hair behind her daughter's ear. "Why don't you take a nap before dinner, Mattie. I'll come wake you up when it's time."

"Okay, Mummy."

"Good girl," Sebastian said as he took the book from her lap and placed it on the nightstand.

Tess removed Mattie's shoes and kissed her on the cheek. "Sweet dreams."

The child closed her eyes and drifted off to sleep. Sebastian and Tess quietly left the room. "She's absolutely brilliant," Sebastian whispered in awe. "That's all from you, Tess."

"She is the best of both of us, Bas."

~ ~ ~ ~

The doctor ordered Penny to bed rest after prescribing a sedative. Sebastian checked in on her to see that she was sleeping soundly. He didn't knock, but slowly opened the door. The bedside lamp was on and Penny lay on her side, grasping Max's pillow. She was still awake.

"May I come in?" he gently inquired.

"Yes."

"Is the sedative helping?"

"I suppose."

Sebastian walked over to Penny and sat on the edge of the bed. Clad in Maxwell's cotton pajama top, she looked exhausted—dark circles under her eyes, her blonde mane pulled back in a messy ponytail.

"Tell me this isn't real, Sebastian."

"I'm so sorry, Pen. I would undo it all if I could."

"I know," she sniffled.

"Lily should be here soon. She wants to make the funeral arrangements. What do you want?"

"Let her do it. I just planned a wedding. How on earth am I going to plan a funeral?" she said, and then burst into tears.

Sebastian lay down on the bed next to her and took her in his arms. "We'll take care of everything. You don't have to worry about anything," he reassured.

A moment later she started to laugh and cry simultaneously. Sebastian looked down at her with a quizzical expression. She must be losing her mind. Grief did do strange things to people, and no two people reacted the same to a tragedy. "It's ironic, isn't it?" she asked.

"What is ironic?"

"Lily kicked you out of the family and you've just become its patriarch. What on earth will she say about that?"

He let what she said sink in for minute. The thought hadn't even occurred to him. *Bollocks, I'm now the Earl of Sutton.* Penny was right—it didn't matter that Lily had disowned him. He'd now inherited an earldom, and it was the very last thing he'd ever wanted.

"Let's not talk of this. You might be pregnant. If you are and have a son, he'll be earl, not me."

"I'm not pregnant. The doctor gave me test."

"I'm so sorry, Pen."

"The world is cruel to give you everything you ever wished for and then snatch it away just as quickly," Penny sighed. "How am I going to go back to the townhouse and be alone? I can't stay here anymore."

"You can stay here as long as you like. This is your home."

"It isn't the same if Max isn't here to share it with me."

"You can stay with Tess and me, if you would like," he said.

"You're sweet to offer, but there isn't enough room." Penny was silent for a moment and then said, "Would you and Tess consider staying with me for a while?"

"Yes, we can do that—as long as you don't mind a rambunctious four-year-old running about the place."

"I welcome the distraction."

Sebastian frowned. He wanted to help her in any way he could. She was his dearest friend. Yet he worried 'the distraction' would only prolong her grieving process. "You need to grieve. Maybe it's not the best idea for us to stay with you."

"You're probably right, but I can't do this alone. I can't even believe this is really happening. I need your support, please," she begged.

"Shh, I'm here for you. Close your eyes. There's plenty of time to talk about this later," Sebastian whispered while stoking her hair.

It took about fifteen minutes, but she finally fell off to sleep. Sebastian carefully maneuvered himself out from under her arm and left her, hopefully to sweet dreams.

When he entered the sitting room, Lily was there, surrounded by Victoria and Sigourney. Tess agreed to stay in their bedroom. He was being overprotective because he had no idea how the encounter would go.

Clearing his throat, he got the women's attention. Lily looked up at him, grief displayed on her face. It was something he had never witnessed before: an emotional Lily.

"How's Penny?" Sigourney asked, trying to keep peace between mother and son.

"She's just fallen asleep."

"We've explained what happened to Mother. Now we're going over arrangements."

Sebastian poured himself a scotch and took the furthest seat away from Lily he could find.

Lily cleared her throat and continued. "As I was saying, I'm make arrangements for funeral service at Westminster Abbey and interment here in the mausoleum."

Sigourney looked over at Sebastian, who sat silently sipping his scotch. He gave a brief nod of the head to let her know he was on board with the plans. "When can we have the service?"

"I'll find out tomorrow when I ring the Archbishop."

"Do you think Penny will approve?" Sigourney asked Sebastian.

"Yes, I think it will be a wonderful way to celebrate Maxwell's life."

Lily gave him a curious look, almost as if she agreed with him. That unnerved Sebastian more than anything.

"I'd like to speak at the funeral," he said.

Lily didn't reply verbally, but gave a curt nod of her head.

Sebastian placed his empty glass on the side table. "You seem to have everything under control here. It's been a very long day. I'm going to bed." With that, he stood and left the room.

"I'll see you in the morning," Sigourney said.

"Goodnight, Sebastian," added Victoria.

Lily said nothing.

Sebastian wearily climbed the stairs and made his way to his and Tess' bedroom. He exhaled a long, heavy breath as he closed the door.

She was waiting up for him, sitting in bed reading. "Well?"

He stepped out of his shoes, pulled off his sweater, and began to unzip his trousers. "This has been the day from hell," he replied, slipping under the covers with Tess.

"And is Lily here?"

"Yes, making plans as we speak."

"Did you talk to her?"

"No, not directly."

"Are we leaving in the morning?"

"Yes, I'd like to leave in the morning."

"What about Penny? I'm worried about her, Bas."

"So am I. She asked if we would move into the townhouse with her. She doesn't want to be alone."

"I think you, of all people, should understand that," Tess said. "If it will help her, then we should do it. I can't imagine the pain she must be in. I can only imagine how I would feel if I lost you. I don't think I could go on." She closed her book and snuggled into his arms.

"Why is life so fragile?" he whispered to her as he closed his eyes and inhaled the scent of her perfume.

"I don't know."

Off-the-cuff he asked, "How do you feel about being a countess?"

The question confused her and she started to chuckle until the realization hit her. "Oh, shit," she said in a very un-Tess-like manner. "You've just become the Earl of Sutton."

"Oh, shit," he repeated, confirming her statement.

She sent out a barrage of questions. "What does this entail, exactly? Do you have to serve in Parliament? Do I have to give up my job at the AP? Do we have to live here?"

He answered the easy questions first. "No, I don't have to get into politics, thank God. No, you don't have to give up your job. No, we don't have to live here, but it is mine now, so it's really up to you. As for what this entails, that's a little more complicated, and a question I don't have the energy to answer right now, okay?"

"Okay."

With that, he turned off the light and pondered how quickly his life had changed in twenty-four hours as Tess drifted off to sleep in his arms.

In the morning Sebastian and Tess persuaded Penny to join them for breakfast. She had managed to shower and dress in jeans and a camel-colored cashmere sweater, but wore no makeup and looked drawn and tired. Mattie held her hand and escorted her to a seat at the table.

Lily, Sigourney, and Victoria were already present, eating their meal. Sebastian made Penny a cup of tea and placed a slice of toast with jam on a china plate for her. Penny nodded her thanks.

Mattie walked over to Lily. "I remember you from the museum," she stated as she stopped in front of her.

"I remember you, too," Lily commented.

"Daddy said you aren't our family. Why are you here?"

"Martha, that's not polite," Sebastian chastised, moving to pull his daughter away from Lily.

Tess grabbed his arm and pulled him back. "Let her go," she said under her breath.

"I'm your grandmother."

Mattie looked at Tess and Sebastian and then looked back at Lily. "I already have a Grandmom Kate. She lives in Pennsylvania."

"You can have two grandmothers," Lily informed the child. "You are correct, however: your father and I aren't family."

"Enough," Sebastian interrupted as he pulled away from Tess and scooped Mattie up in his arms. His eyes bored into Lily. "I will be civil to you for Maxwell's sake, but that is all." Turning on his heel, he walked Mattie to the other end of the table and sat her down next to Penny. "Eat your eggs so we can go home, Martha."

Lily delicately wiped her mouth with the linen napkin and stood from the table. She walked over to Penny and said, "I'm sorry for your loss. When you finish breakfast, I'd like to speak to you privately in my office regarding the funeral arrangements."

Penny glanced up at her mother-in-law and nodded her head in agreement. Lily left the room.

"What the hell!" Sebastian seethed, hitting the table with his fist.

"Daddy, no bad language," Mattie chided.

Sebastian took a deep breath, counting to ten to gain his composure. "I'm sorry, darling."

"How can she be my grandmom?" Mattie asked, still confused.

"It's a complicated story, Mattie. I'll try to explain when we get home, okay?" Tess said.

Mattie shrugged her shoulders and tucked into her eggs and toast.

"That went well, all things considered," Sigourney piped in from the other end of the table.

It was bad enough they had to bury Max; now he had to deal with Lily, too. Sebastian wondered if he had the strength to get through it. The sound of Penny pushing her plate away jolted him from his thoughts.

"I can't eat," she sighed. "Let me go get this over with and then we can leave."

"You're going back to London?" Sigourney questioned.

"I can't stay here—not without Maxwell," Penny solemnly replied.

"I'll have your things packed up and sent down for you," Sigourney offered.

"Thank you, Sigourney. I would appreciate that very much."

"I'll come with you," Sebastian said, reaching for her hand.

"No, I'm fine. Stay here with your family."

Sebastian pushed his plate back and watched Penny leave the room.

# Chapter 24 - I Know It's Over

Maxwell's funeral took place on Thursday. Sebastian escorted Penny, who wore a black silk dress. A matching fascinator perched atop her head contained a small veil that just covered her eyes. Next, he walked Tess and Mattie to the same church pew and they took their seats next to Penny. Lady Lily Irons sat across the aisle, somber and retrospective, with Sigourney and Victoria. Thankfully, they couldn't see the two thousand people in attendance, since they were sitting behind them with only a view of the closed coffin bearing the Earl of Sutton's coat of arms. Penny held tight to one of Maxwell's handkerchiefs as the service began.

The service started with hymns and prayers, and then it was Sebastian's turn to speak. He slowly walked to the podium, past his brother's casket, holding a letter in his right hand. When he reached the podium, Sebastian cleared his throat. "Growing up, I never knew my brother, Maxwell. He was ten years older than I am, and it wasn't until my family and I moved back to London that we began to have a relationship. I was hesitant to make the first move, but all the women in my life said the same thing: Max is a good man. Whether he was running an electronics company or fundraising for a charity or doting on his loving wife and niece, he was always caring, honorable, and loving." Sebastian took a deep breath to calm his nerves and slowly exhaled. "My biggest regret is that he never had the child he longed for with Penelope. It's cruel that his life ended without that dream being fulfilled. Life is unexpected and too short. Max lived his life to the fullest, and I just wanted to remind everyone of that fact. Try not to weep, but rejoice in the life he lead. Maxwell Irons was indeed a good man."

Sebastian carefully folded his paper and stepped away from the podium. He took his place in the front row, sitting between Tess and Penny. Poor Penny, numb and silent, her eyes emoting so much grief that Sebastian couldn't bear to look at her. He offered his hand and Penny accepted, curling her long, delicate fingers around his for strength.

The ceremony lasted an hour. In the end, the minister said a prayer: "Heavenly Father, please take

Maxwell Irons into your loving arms. We thank you for the memories of Maxwell, which we can keep as a source of comfort and continuing thankfulness. We ask this through Jesus Christ our Lord, Amen."

The recessional music began to play as the pallbearers, including Sebastian, lifted his brother's coffin and walked the long aisle to exit the Abbey. The casket was slowly placed in the hearse as the mourners flowed out of the building.

Sebastian glanced around the crowd to locate his family and Penny. The one person he never expected to see was his father, Martin Christopher Baker, standing on the sidewalk near the gothic pillar, in a black suit and tie. Shocked, Sebastian froze and blinked his eyes to make sure it wasn't a mirage. Martin approached. Sebastian finally managed to speak a few words. "What are you doing here?"

"I wanted to be at my son's funeral," Martin simply replied. Then he quickly added, "I'm sorry how we left things in Greece. I'd like to make it up to you."

Sebastian shook his head. "I can't do this right now. We're taking Max to the castle to bury him."

"May I come?" Martin asked, with an eager look in his eyes.

"Lily will be there," he muttered, dreading the nuclear disaster that could occur if Martin set foot on the property again.

"He's my son, too. I deserve to be there."

"Suit yourself," Sebastian acquiesced. "I assume you remember the way."

Martin dipped his head and then turned and walked away. Sebastian scanned the throng of people once more to find Tess, but she found him first. Alistair was escorting the two women and Mattie in his direction. "Are we ready to go?" Sebastian asked.

"Yes," Tess replied. The girls walked to the limo and got inside.

Sebastian pulled Alistair back. "Can you come up to the castle with me for the burial?"

"Are you sure Penny would want me there?"

"I'm not worried about Penny—it's my father and Lily that have me concerned."

Alistair turned his head to his side and raised an eyebrow.

"Don't ask. I just need backup."

"I'll follow in my car," Alistair agreed without further questioning.

As soon as Sebastian got in the back seat of the limo, they were off. Mattie's black taffeta skirt made a crinkling sound as she sat on his lap and placed her head on his shoulder. "I'm sad, Daddy," she said in a small, quiet voice.

"So am I, darling." He glanced over at Tess, who was holding Penny's hand. From time to time, Penny would dab a stray tear with the handkerchief she held.

No one said another word the entire ride out to the castle. When they arrived, the casket was removed by the liveried footmen and the cortege of mourners followed the casket along the pebbled pathway leading to the mausoleum.

A few final prayers were said, and then Maxwell's coffin was slid into the wall space next to his grandfather. Penny turned her head in to Sebastian's shoulder, unable to watch. Alistair stood behind Tess and Mattie, a hand on each of their shoulders. Lily stood stoic and proud. Sigourney and Victoria shed a few tears.

Sebastian nervously looked over his shoulder for Martin. He found the man standing several feet back in the doorway. In that exact same moment, Lady Irons turned around and noticed him, too.

In a flash, Lily walked with purpose toward the exit. She grabbed Martin by the suit coat and pulled him outside the mausoleum. Victoria and Sigourney looked over, confused, for they only saw the man's back and didn't realize it was their father.

"Damn it," Sebastian muttered under his breath. He tapped Alistair on the shoulder and the two men followed Lily and Martin.

They rounded the corner of the stone structure and found Lily and Martin standing in the field having a row. "How dare you step foot on this property again!"

"I've stayed away from my children for twenty-five years, no thanks to you. Enough is enough!"

"You stayed away because my monthly payments to your bank account were more important to you than your children," she seethed, her eyes brimming with hatred.

"You always were a bitch, Lily. I see that has not changed."

"And you were always the philandering husband who couldn't keep your trousers zipped!"

Sebastian couldn't help it: he laughed aloud. Never had he witnessed his mother speak in this manner, and it was equal parts pathetic and comical.

Martin and Lily stopped their feud and turned toward the sound of the laughter. Lily held her head high and straightened her suit jacket. Martin put his hands in his pockets.

"As amusing as this little scene is, it is not the place nor the time to air your dirty laundry. Have some respect for the dead, will you?" Sebastian intervened.

By now the ladies had all come out of the mausoleum. Mattie walked up to Sebastian and said, "Daddy, who's that man?"

"That's your grandfather, Mattie."

"Is he our family?"

"That remains to be seen yet. It's cold out here. Come, everyone, we should go inside. The staff prepared a luncheon."

The group began to make their way along the path back up to the castle—everyone except Lily and Martin and Sebastian.

"You are not stepping foot in that house while I'm still breathing," Lily threatened.

"Technically, it's no longer your house, Lily," Sebastian reminded her with a smug grin.

"I've disowned you. You have nothing to do with this."

"I have everything to do with this. Max is dead. I'm now the Earl of Sutton, in case you've forgotten." The remark effectively stunned her into silence. Martin chuckled this time. Sebastian turned and leveled an angry glare at him. "You are not exactly my favorite person at the moment, either. You have some nerve deciding to make your return at Max's funeral."

Martin moved to speak, but Sebastian silenced him with his hand. "Now, you are both welcome to join me for lunch, but you better be on your best behavior. If you make a scene, I'll think nothing of having you both thrown out on your arse." Sebastian didn't wait for a response and started walking toward the house. To his surprise, Lily and Martin fell in line behind him.

# Chapter 25 - Break My Heart

Common sense and good manners won out over a knock-down, drag-out family squabble for the time being. Lily sat at the head of the table at one end while Sebastian sat at the opposite end. Martin sat to Sebastian's left, as far away from Lily as possible. Sebastian didn't have much of an appetite. Instead, he spent his time pushing the food around his plate and watching the others seated at the table. Lily busied herself with quiet conversation between Sigourney and Victoria. He didn't know if he had the strength to deal with any of this, but he also knew he didn't have a choice. Like it or not, he was now head of the Irons family and the job came with great responsibility.

Penny took a few bites of her food and then placed the sterling silver fork on the plate. "Sebastian, this was lovely, but I need some air. Can you please excuse me?"

"Do you want me to come with you?" he asked.

"I've got it," Alistair chimed in, already standing from his chair and helping Penny rise from her seat.

Penny silently glanced at Alistair, but bowed her head in agreement. The two of them left the dining room.

"Sebastian, I'd like a word and then I'll be on my way," Martin said.

"Fine," Sebastian agreed. "Excuse me, everyone."

They walked to the sitting room. Martin entered first and Sebastian followed, closing the doors behind him. Martin walked over to the fireplace and studied the painting above the mantel—a Dutch still-life of various fruits on a wooden table, the colors dark and muted. "I always hated that painting," he admitted.

"Why are you here?" Sebastian asked.

"I wanted to attend my son's funeral."

"Maxwell wasn't very fond of you."

"I deserted him when he was ten years old. How could he be?" Martin agreed, turning to face Sebastian.

Sebastian poured a scotch and offered it to Martin, who gratefully accepted. "How did you know he died?" Sebastian inquired, sipping his own glass.

"I pay someone here in London to keep tabs on you children. They report back to me. It was the only way I could stay in touch—"

"And still keep your stipend?" Sebastian cut in.

Martin bowed his head in embarrassment. "Yes. I'd be damned if I was going to back to teaching rich old women to play tennis. I'd become accustomed to a certain way of living. I wasn't willing to give that up."

"I can't believe you just admitted that aloud," Sebastian said.

"It's the truth."

"And the truth isn't always pretty," Sebastian muttered to himself, recalling the conversation he'd had with Tess all those years ago when he'd tried to explain how he lived his life as a Libertine. "You've lost your stipend now. Lily will cut you off."

"I know."

"How sad it took the death of your child to make you come to your senses."

"It wasn't Max's death. It was you, actually," Martin declared, looking him in the eye.

"Me? I don't understand."

"You were so much like me, Sebastian. Wealthy playboy, outrageous parties, getting kicked out of Eton—you were the ultimate party boy. And then you disappeared for a few years and my man didn't have any information on you."

"I was in America."

"You changed your life around. You became a man—someone I'm proud to call my son. When you turned up in Corfu with your wife and I saw how responsible and refined you'd become, I started to wonder if maybe I could make amends and become a better man."

Sebastian stared at Martin. He was gobsmacked, unsure he had just heard the words come out of his father's mouth. "Wait—you knew about me! You pretended to not know who I was in Corfu. You said you didn't know Lily was pregnant when you left."

"I lied. It was a shock to see you standing on my doorstep. I didn't know why you would track me down."

Without thinking, Sebastian made a fist and threw a punch at his father, landing the hit square on his jaw. The crystal glass Martin was holding crashed to the ground and shattered into tiny pieces. "What about the comment you made in Corfu? The one about when I grow up someday I'll understand?" he questioned with disdain.

Martin opened his jaw and worked it in a circle to confirm it wasn't broken. "Life is complicated, Sebastian."

"I'm fucking aware of that fact, Martin," he growled.

"I've handled this poorly. I admit it. Max's death shook me to the core. I want to make amends, Sebastian. I want my children back in my life."

"And what if we don't want you back in our lives?"

"Then I will accept it and know that I tried. I could hardly blame any of you for turning me away," Martin admitted, defeated.

It seemed they were at an impasse—Martin asking forgiveness and Sebastian unsure he could grant it. The door creaked as it opened, gaining Sebastian's attention. Tess was standing in the doorway, dressed in black, looking beautiful as ever. The corner of his lips curved up at the sight of her. Seeing her made his anger instantly disappear.

"I guess I'll be going," Martin said, breaking the silence. He began to leave the room.

"Where are you staying in London?"

"Grosvenor House."

"I'll talk to Victoria and Sigourney. If they have any interest in hearing what you have to say, we'll meet you tomorrow at noon in the lobby," Sebastian informed him.

"Thank you, Sebastian."

Martin walked past Tess and gave her a feeble smile. Then he was gone.

Tess looked at the fireplace and noticed the pieces of glass and amber liquor on the floor. "Are you okay?" she gingerly asked, reaching for her husband's hand.

He let out the heavy breath he'd been holding in—it sounded like a cross between a weary sigh and a chuckle. "I'm so tired, Tess. All I want to do is get pissed and smoke a cigarette," he confessed.

"Neither one of those things is good for you."

"I know," he agreed, sitting down on the sofa and propping his feet up on the antique coffee table. Tess sat next to him. "How is it that I've become a more responsible adult than my parents?"

"I don't know." Pointing to the shattered glass on floor, Tess asked, "What was that all about?"

"Martin admitted he knew about me all along. I punched him," he replied matter-of-factly.

"What?"

Sebastian merely shrugged, at a loss for words.

"Why can't anything ever be simple with your family?"

"I've asked myself that question for years and I still don't have the answer." Sebastian stood from the sofa and offered his hand to Tess. "Let's find Penny and go home."

~ ~ ~ ~

Penny and Alistair walked together, keeping a proper length distance from one another. "Thank you for coming to the funeral today. You didn't have to do that," Penny said as she looked out upon the horizon.

"I wanted to show my support. I liked Maxwell. We belonged to the same club."

"I *loved* Maxwell."

"I know." Alistair stopped and shuffled his feet of the stone path. "Things didn't end so well for you and me. I'm truly sorry for that. I'd like to be friends again, if you're willing to try."

Penny had walked ahead, but stopped and turned to face him. "I could certainly use all the friends I can get right now," she acknowledged.

"Can I call on you for tea some afternoon?"

"Sebastian and his family are staying with me right now. Yes, it would be nice for you to stop by. Mattie loves her tea parties," she added, almost breaking into a grin.

"That little one is something else. Sebastian seemed to be the wildest of us all—and now, looking at him today, the transformation is astonishing," Alistair commented, scratching his head.

"Sebastian was lucky enough to find his soul mate."

"There you are," Sebastian called out from behind them. "Are you ready to go, Pen?"

"Yes."

The three of them began walking back to the house, entering through the back door. Tess and Mattie were waiting with their coats on. Surprisingly, Lily, Victoria, and Sigourney were there as well.

"We still need to talk, Sebastian," Lily said, her gray eyes cold and void of emotion.

"Not now. We can talk after the will is read at the solicitor's office on Wednesday." The confidence with which he spoke seemed to take Lily by surprise, and she didn't speak another word. He turned toward his sisters. "Tomorrow at noon?"

"Yes," they replied in unison.

# Chapter 26 - The Truth

Penny sat in the lounge chair, dressed in black trousers and a cashmere turtleneck sweater. The latest issue of *Vogue* sat open on her lap in her meager attempt to feign interest in something other than her own grief.

Mattie walked into the room, dressed in her school uniform and ready to start the day. She was carrying a china plate with a scone and a side of clotted cream. "Aunt Penny, I made you breakfast," she gleefully announced, walking to toward her.

"Why did you do that?"

"You're not eating. You look tired and need energy," the child replied.

"Perhaps you're right. Will you sit with me and share it?"

"I had cereal for breakfast, but I'll sit with you. Daddy should be here soon to take me to school. Will you come with us, please?"

No matter how much Penny didn't feel like eating or going out in public, she couldn't say no to the little girl. "Yes, I'll take you to school."

"Yay!" Mattie spied the open issue of *Vogue* on Penny's lap. "Can I look at this while you eat your breakfast?"

"Of course."

Mattie sat on the floor, pulled the magazine onto the ottoman, and started flipping through the pages. Sebastian entered the room in his usual suit and tie. He smiled to himself as he watched Penny finally eat some solid food, Mattie keeping her company. "Good morning," he announced.

"Hi, Daddy."

"Are you almost ready to head to school?"

"When Aunt Penny finishes her breakfast, we can go."

Tess entered the room. "Mattie, you better get ready to go," she said, putting on her coat. "I might run a little late tonight. I'll call you from the office," she directed to her husband. "I love you. Good luck today." Tess gave him a quick kiss on the lips. "Mattie—hugs?"

Mattie ran over to her mum and gave her a hug. "Have a good day, Mummy."

"You too. I love you." She waved to Penny. "Call me if you need anything." Tess grabbed her briefcase and was gone.

Penny placed the empty plate on the coffee table. "Finished. Now let's get you to school. You heard your mother—you shouldn't be tardy."

They took a cab across town and dropped Mattie at school.

"Let's grab some coffees and take a walk in the park," Sebastian suggested.

"Lead the way," Penny agreed.

Sebastian popped into Pret A Manger and purchased two coffees with cream and sugar. They walked down the block and entered the quaint little park through wrought-iron gates. The leaves on the trees were brown, but still hanging onto their branches.

"I'm sorry about all the excitement at the castle yesterday. I could have strangled Lily and Martin for causing a scene."

Penny brushed off the comment with a wave of her hand. "It wasn't your fault, Sebastian."

"I'm still raving mad at them."

"Are you going to meet Martin today? Sigourney told me what happened. She's eager to speak with him and get his side of the story."

"He's a liar. I'm not sure I can believe a word that comes out of his mouth. At the same time, I don't want Sigourney and Victoria to go it alone."

The corner of her lip turned up slightly. It was the first remnant of a smile he had seen in over a week. "Always the protector—it's one of the things I love about you, Sebastian."

"I swear if I could turn back time, I would change everything for you."

"But you can't. I appreciate that you want to, though." Penny exhaled, her hot breath turning to fog as it hit the cold November air. She took a seat on a nearby wooden bench. "I had six months with Max. Everything was so wonderful. Why did it have to end?"

He wanted to say 'maybe the best hasn't happened yet,' but that sounded crass and cliché, even to him. Why did Tess' father have to drop dead of a heart attack when she was only fourteen? There was no reason. That's the way it was, and this was no comfort at all. "I don't know the answer, Pen."

She looked down at the diamond and platinum engagement ring that Maxwell had given her, admiring its beauty. She set the half empty coffee cup on the bench and then removed the ring from her finger. Turning over Sebastian's hand, she placed the ring in his palm.

"What are you doing?" he asked.

"This is yours now. It's a family heirloom. I'll have no children to pass it on to. It belongs to the Earl of Sutton. Maybe one day you and Tess will have a son."

"Penny…"

"Please take it, Sebastian," she pleaded, cutting him off. "You know I'm right. The longer I wear it, the harder it will be to take it off. I need to find the strength to move on."

"Oh, Pen," he muttered, placing his arm around her shoulder and pulling her close to his body.

"We should be going if you're going to make your meeting."

"Will you be okay?"

"I have to be okay, don't I?"

The lobby of the Grosvenor House Hotel was opulent yet understated. The marble floor was shined to perfection. A large round mahogany table displayed an elegant floral arrangement. Sebastian noticed Victoria and Sigourney sitting in the plush red velvet chairs next to the fireplace. They looked up as he approached. Glancing at this Rolex, he noticed the time: it was noon. As if on cue, Martin Christopher Baker exited the lift and walked over to meet them.

"Thank you for meeting me," Martin said, rubbing his thumb against his palm.

"We're curious to hear what you have to say," Sigourney announced.

"Maybe we could move into the bar and sit at a table."

"Fine by me," Sebastian muttered, eager for a scotch even though it was only noon.

They sat at a round table with high-backed seats to give them privacy. The girls ordered mimosas while Martin requested scotch—neat. Sebastian begrudgingly ordered the same. After the drinks were delivered, Martin was the first to take a sip. He glanced up at his children and sighed. "I'm sorry for Max's loss. It's never easy to see someone die young, and it is even harder when it's your child."

Victoria almost snorted her champagne in a very unladylike manner. "Pardon me, but you made the decision to leave us. I don't think you have any right to mourn or ask for our sympathy."

Sebastian sat back in his seat, surprised by his sister's outburst. She sounded a little too much like Lily, and it unnerved him. The only consolation was that Sebastian actually agreed with Victoria.

Martin wearily ran his fingers through his graying hair. "I am truly sorry for the pain I caused you children. I didn't want to leave you. I had no choice."

"You always have a choice," Victoria seethed.

"I wish there was a way to turn back time, but what's done is done."

"Precisely. And I choose not to listen to your excuses anymore. What you did only shows you are a coward, and I have no respect for you." With that, Victoria stood from the table and left the room.

Martin turned his attention to Sigourney. She gazed back, her mouth in a hard line and her eyes unreadable.

"I've not been a perfect father, Sigourney. I know this. I'm just asking for an opportunity to get you know again." He swallowed hard and extended his hand. "Hello, I'm Martin."

Sigourney reached for his hand and accepted his greeting. "Hello, Martin."

Sebastian smiled at his sister. She always was the easygoing one—the peacemaker; it didn't surprise him that she would be the one to extend the olive branch.

"So tell me about your life, Martin?" she asked with great curiosity.

And so Martin began to tell the story of how he became an ex-pat, living in Greece, meeting his partner, Colette. He admitted that he kept tabs on the children as they grew, attended university, and sought careers. He finished his scotch as he finished his commentary and pushed the glass away. "Victoria was right: I am a coward and I do have a choice. I want to make this up to you both, if you'll give me the chance."

"That's a little difficult to do from Corfu," Sebastian reminded.

Sigourney reached over and touched Sebastian's hand. "Everyone deserves a second chance, Sebastian."

Sebastian conceded with a nod of his head. He had changed his life, and it wouldn't have happened without people who were willing to give him the opportunity to change. Maybe now was the time to pay it forward and give someone else the benefit of the doubt. Sebastian leaned forward and shook Martin's hand. "It's nice to meet you, Martin."

# Chapter 27 - Conflicting Emotions

Sebastian and Tess lay in bed talking about their day. "I miss you guys," Tess admitted. "I'm sorry things have been so crazy at the office and I have to work late. Thank God I have you to take care of Mattie."

"Are you happy?"

"I'm happy. I just miss you." She snuggled closer. "I worry about you, Bas. With everything that is happening: Max, your father, the earldom…Are you happy?"

"As long as I have you and Mattie, I'm happy." He kissed the top of her head. "I do admit I'm feeling a little overwhelmed at the moment."

"How so?"

"The will is read tomorrow. Martin wants absolution. Penny is grieving. I have to make a decision on what to do with Max's office and secretary. Ugh, I could really use your organizational skills right now. I don't see any way to handle this other than to quit my job at the gallery."

"But you love it there!" she exclaimed, propping her head up on her hand to make eye contact with her husband.

"I suppose I'll know more after tomorrow. I have no idea what it takes to run an estate and support the charities that Max did. How can I possibly do it all and care for Mattie? I won't hire a Nanny, Tess. You know how I feel about that."

"I wish I could go with you to meet the lawyer tomorrow."

"You've missed too much work already. I'll be fine."

Tess tilted her head and kissed Sebastian on the lips. "It seems the only time we get to talk anymore is in bed, late at night."

He let out a long, slow breath and his chest contracted under Tess' touch. "We'll figure this out, right?"

"Of course we will. We've dealt with worse. We can handle this, too," she reassured him.

"Martin and Colette want to have dinner at The Ivy before they fly out on Saturday. Do you think you can make an eight o'clock dinner on Friday night? I've asked Penny if she'd watch Mattie."

"Yes, I should be able to do that. I can always work on Saturday. Are you sure it's a good thing to leave Mattie with Penny?"

"I think it's probably the best thing for her right now. Pen interacts with Mattie and Mattie gets her to eat. They've become quite the team."

"How much longer do you think we should stay here in her house? I want to be here to support in any way I can, but I miss our home."

"I know, darling. I need to talk with Pen. I'll do it tomorrow after the will reading."

At ten o'clock the next day, Lily, Sebastian, Victoria, Sigourney, and Penny sat in the lawyer's conference room awaiting the reading of the will. It brought back memories of Nanny, and Sebastian longed to have Tess by his side, but she was at work. There was no time for self-pity; Penny needed him to be strong. The lawyer shuffled into the room, impeccably dressed in a gray pinstriped suit and flanked by an assistant.

"Thank you all for coming," he said, sitting down at the head of the table and opening a file. Without further ado, he began to read the will.

All shares of Irons Electronics where bequeathed to Victoria. This now made her equal partners with

Lily. Sebastian was more than grateful to not have anything to do with the company, and it was fitting for Victoria to have them since she would one day run the company.

Lily was bequeathed the Mayfair townhouse. Sigourney was bequeathed the cottage in the South of France.

As the lawyer began to read the part of the will that involved Penny, she nervously reached for Sebastian's hand. "To my loving wife Penelope, I leave the sum of one million pounds."

Lily held her head high, annoyed at the announcement.

Penny leaned her head on Sebastian's shoulder. "I'd rather have Max back instead of the money," she softly whispered to Sebastian.

"Lastly, to Sebastian Irons, I bequeath Sutton Castle, my collection of cars, all heirlooms and family positions of the Earl of Sutton, and the sum of three million pounds to run the estate and care for its workers."

Sebastian's mouth opened in disbelief. If Lily seemed annoyed before, now she looked downright indignant. Penny glanced at Sebastian and gave him a slight smile while squeezing his hand.

The lawyer had papers for each person to sign and then they were free to go. Sebastian almost made it out the exit before Lily cornered him. "You must be very pleased," she said, her voice dripping with disdain.

"I'm not pleased at all. I never wanted any of this, but now it's my responsibility." He buttoned his coat as the cold December air blew through the open door. "You can have a wing of the castle, but I don't want you to step foot on the grounds when I'm there. I'll have Max's secretary ring your secretary to set up a schedule."

"You can't do this to me. Sutton castle is my home."

"It's my home now, and you are no longer welcome there when my family is present. If you can't live with that, I'll call a mover today and have your things removed at once," he coolly replied. Threading Penny's arm though his, he said, "Are you ready to go?"

She silently nodded and they walked out onto the street and hailed a cab before Lily could utter another word.

Inside the warm cab, Penny turned to Sebastian and said, "I'm so sorry this all falls on you now."

He shrugged, resigned to his fate. "Would you be up to helping me sort through all this mess? The estate, the charities, the staff—you must have some idea how to handle it." He sighed and then quickly added, "But if it's too painful, I understand."

"Of course I'll help you. What else do I have to do?" she replied, full of melancholy. "By the way you just put Lily in her place, you'll be fine."

It was a short cab ride to Westminster and Max's office. They disembarked and entered the building. Max's secretary was dutifully seated at her desk, opening correspondence. Sebastian didn't know if he would continue to need an assistant but didn't want to put the poor woman out of a job, so he kept her on—business as usual. "Mr. Irons and Mrs. Irons, can I get you some tea or coffee?"

"Tea, please," Penny replied.

"Same here," Sebastian agreed. "After tea, we need to talk about Max's schedule. Bring your notes and calendar."

The secretary nodded and began collecting the information while Sebastian and Penny walked into Max's office. Taking the seat behind Max's desk, he looked out over the desktop, neat and organized, with no clutter. That was Max. His wedding photo stood on the corner in a sterling silver frame, recalling happier times. "If there is anything here you want to take, Pen, it's yours."

She picked up the photo and smiled. "That was the best day of my life. Do you ever think I'll be happy again?"

"Yes, I do. It may not be right away, but I think you will find happiness again," he replied in all earnest.

"Then I just have to believe that, or there's no point in going on," she murmured.

The secretary entered the room with a tea service and poured them each a cup. Sebastian thanked her. Pulling the calendar on Max's desk in front of him, he picked up a pen and prepared for the onslaught of note-taking.

Two hours later, his head was spinning. They'd covered the charities Max chaired and the causes they supported. Penny was a big help with information on this front. Sebastian was astounded by the information regarding the castle and grounds—the upkeep and bills and the staff. He would definitely be leaving his job at the gallery. Running the castle seemed like running a small corporation, and the cost was astronomical. No wonder Max left him three million pounds to run it. The next call Sebastian would have to make was to Mr. Hume to have him run over the financials and see if there was any way he could invest the money to make a profit and keep the staff employed for many years to come.

Later that evening, Sebastian took Mattie to McDonald's for dinner because Tess was working late again. They sat in a booth, eating cheeseburgers. "Did you have a good day, Daddy?"

"Not particularly, Mattie. Did you enjoy your play date with Michael after school?"

"Yes," she replied, sipping her milk. "Why are you sad?"

"I miss Uncle Max. I feel bad for Aunt Penny. Now that Uncle Max is gone, I have to take over his job."

"So you have to take Aunt Penny to charity balls now?"

Sebastian looked at his daughter and smiled. *Oh, if it were only that simple.* Someday she would understand. Hell, she'd have a front row seat. "No, Mattie. I now own the castle and need to take care of the people who work there."

"We get to live in the castle!" she exclaimed.

"Only on the weekends, when you aren't in school," Sebastian explained.

"I want to live there now. Can't I go to another school?"

"Wouldn't you miss your friend Michael?"

The child pouted. "Yes."

"I not sure what we'll do next. I have to talk to Mummy about it."

"She gives good advice."

"That she does," he agreed. "Now finish your meal so we can get home."

# Chapter 28 - By My Side

Tess walked through the front door of Penny's townhouse around nine o'clock in the evening. Exhausted, she set her briefcase on the floor in the hallway and walked into the parlor. She found Sebastian poring over documents and a notebook.

He looked up when she entered the room. "Hello, darling."

"Hey," she replied with a smile as she walked over to join him on the sofa. Looking down at the papers, she grimaced. "That looks menacing."

"I'm not having much fun, I can vouch for that."

"What is all this?"

"Max's info regarding a dozen charities, the household budget for the castle, and a list of its employees and job descriptions."

"I'm so sorry," she whispered. Tess grabbed all the paperwork from his hands and placed it on the coffee table. Next, she sat on her husband's lap and wrapped her arms around his neck. "I love you."

He kissed her, and in that one move he found solace. The kiss deepened; their tongues caressed in a slow, languid motion. Pulling apart with a labored breath, he said, "I don't want to talk right now. I just want to make love to you."

"Hmm, that sounds wonderful." Tess stood from her husband's lap and took his hand, escorting him up the stairs to their temporary bedroom.

Inside their cozy room, they undressed one other. Piece by piece, the layers were stripped until they were naked. "I've missed you so much," he murmured, running his hand down her spine until he reached had cupped her gorgeous ass. Next he walked her backwards until the backs of her knees hit the edge of the mattress.

Tess sat down and dragged her fingertips along his well-defined, smooth chest. "I miss you more," she told him before leaning in and kissing the tip of his erection.

"I like that. It feels so good." Sebastian tilted his head back and closed his eyes, concentrating on the heady sensation of her lips that were now wrapped around his cock. Between the exhaustion and the excitement he was feeling, Sebastian wasn't sure how much longer he could remain standing. He pulled away from his wife and moved her body to the center of the bed. Lying of top on her, he kissed her jaw and then moved along her neck and then down to her breasts, licking, nipping, and kneading them until Tess let out a low moan that let him know he was having the desired effect.

"Please—now," she pleaded, knotting her fingers through the hair at the nape of his neck.

His mind wandered back to the time they first lived together and their spectacular honeymoon, when sex was something they seemed to do every day. Now sex was infrequent and quick because life just seemed to take over. He granted her request and eased inside her. Tess was his *home,* and as long as he remembered this, everything else would work itself out. Tess let out a short, quick gasp, and then he felt her muscles tighten around his cock as she climaxed. Feeling her come undone around him sent him over the edge.

Tess let out a small yawn that she covered with her hand. "So tired," she said, wrapping her arms around her husband as he lay his head on her breast.

"Sleep now, Tess."

The alarm clock buzzed incessantly and Sebastian blindly reached over and hit it with the palm of his hand to turn it off. Tess squirmed underneath him, unhappy to have her slumber disturbed.

"Darling, get up. We need to shower," Sebastian coaxed with a little nudge.

"Hmm—together?" she asked in a quiet voice as she slowly opened her eyes.

"Can't think of a better way to start the day, can you?"

Tess sat up in bed and stretched her hands above her head, the white sheet falling onto her lap, revealing her naked breasts. "Okay."

"You keep that up and I'll ring the office and tell them you are sick so we can spend the day in bed," he threatened.

"That sounds like heaven," she wistfully replied, getting out of bed. "But we have your father's dinner tonight and we need to get Mattie off to school."

"No-nonsense Hamilton returns," he pouted, also getting out of bed.

They walked into the bathroom and Tess started the shower. She stepped in first, and Sebastian followed. Taking the handheld shower nozzle from her, he began to wet her skin and then her hair.

"Aren't you tired of all the responsibility? Don't you ever just want to say dash it all and be free?"

"It a lovely thought, Bas, but it's not realistic." Tess took the shower nozzle from her husband and began to wet his skin.

"I know," he muttered, relaxing under the stream of hot water. "I feel like the bloody mayor of London, complete with budgets and payrolls. I wish we were back in New York."

Tess placed the shower nozzle back in its holder and wrapped her arms around Sebastian. "I can help you look over everything this weekend. We can make a schedule. That might help."

Shaking his head, he grinned. Tess and her schedules seemed to be the answer to everything. "I could use all the help I can get right now. Thank you."

"What do you have planned for today?" she asked, taking the loofah and scrubbing his back.

"I've got to ring Fiona and tell her the news. I'm going to need to leave the gallery, but I'm hoping she'll let me stay on as a consultant."

"Fiona adores you—I'm sure that won't be a problem."

"Next I have go meet with Mr. Hume and go over Max's finances to see if there is a better way to invest the money so we can keep the castle going."

"I wish I could go with you. I'm so sorry you have to do this alone."

Turning around to face his wife, he leaned in and kissed her forehead. "I wish you could be there, too. We'll talk at length this weekend, okay?"

Sebastian stood in front of the mirror fixing his tie while Tess sat on the bed putting on her shoes. When she finished, she walked up behind her husband. Placing her hands on his shoulders, she said, "You look very handsome."

He glanced at her maroon dress and black heels. "You look amazing, as always."

"I dressed extra nice—just in case I run late at work, I can meet you directly at The Ivy.

"Have a good day at work."

Tess gave him a quick kiss on the lips. "Penny is still okay with watching Mattie?"

"Yes, we're good to go."

"Love you."

"Love you, too."

With that, Tess turned to the right and headed toward the stairs while Sebastian turned to the left to wake Mattie. Opening the door to her bedroom, he peeked inside. She was already awake and dressing for school.

"Look at you, up and ready."

"Hi, Daddy. Can we go to the castle this weekend?"

"I don't know, darling. I have a dinner tonight and I have paperwork to do this weekend."

"Can't you do it at the castle?"

His child was too logical for her own good—and she certainly hadn't inherited that trait from him. "Let me talk to your mum tonight. We if go, it won't be until tomorrow morning."

Satisfied with his response, Mattie took his hand. "Let's eat."

# Chapter 29 - Changes

Tess made it to The Ivy with five minutes to spare. Sebastian was waiting outside, pacing the sidewalk. "Sorry, to cut it so close," she apologized and then kissed him on the cheek.

"It's bloody freezing out here. Let's go inside," he said, opening the door for her to enter first.

The waitress walked them over to a table at the center of the room, where the rest of the party was seated. Sigourney, Martin, and Colette had already started in on the wine. Sebastian pulled out a chair for Tess and then he sat down.

"I'm so glad we could all get together before Martin and I fly back to Greece," Colette announced.

"It is nice to see you again," Tess added.

Over the course of the two-hour meal, Sigourney, Tess, and Sebastian took turns telling Martin about their lives. Martin had a genuine interest in their tales, and Sebastian thought maybe there could be a reconciliation after all. The evening was drama-free and no one raised their voice in anger. It was a welcome change of pace.

The group parted ways outside the restaurant and filed into separate cabs.

"That went better than I expected," Sebastian said, loosening his tie as the cab drove toward Kensington.

"Martin seemed sincere," Tess added.

"Yes, he did. Did you get all your work finished today?"

"Yes, that's why I was close to being late."

"Mattie wants to go to the castle tomorrow."

"I think we should go, Bas. I want to help you with budgets and payroll. I think going there in person would be the best place to do it. This way you can talk to the person in charge. I'm sure he'll be able to give you insights into how the household is run."

Sebastian looked at his wife. The night lights flitted across her face as the cab moved down the street. A mixture of pride, love, and relief swelled in his heart. "You have no idea how much I need you," he softly said, reaching for her hand.

"I do know," she smiled. "I need you just as much."

In the morning, Sebastian had all the bags packed in the back of Max's Range Rover. Penny was sitting in the parlor, reading the newspaper.

"We're almost ready to go. Are you sure you don't want to come along?" he asked.

"No, I'm not ready yet."

"I feel bad leaving you alone, Pen."

"I'll be fine." She folded the paper and placed it on the coffee table. "You, Tess, and Mattie have been so supportive these past few weeks. I'm so very grateful, but you need to get back to living your lives and I need to figure out how to move forward in mine. When you come back to London, you don't have to stay here. I'm sure you miss your flat and your daily routine."

"I do," Sebastian admitted.

Penny stood from the chair and hugged Sebastian. "You have been a brilliant friend. I will never forget this."

"I'm a phone call away if you need *anything*." He pulled away and caressed her cheek. "I best go round up Tess and Mattie."

"Have a nice weekend, Sebastian."

Sebastian entered the kitchen and found Tess cleaning up the dirty dishes. "Almost ready to go," she said, placing the last bowl on the dish rack to dry.

"Where's Mattie?"

"I thought she was with you."

Sebastian huffed in exasperation. "She wanted to go and now she disappears."

Tess laid the towel on the counter. Then she walked over to her husband and gave him a hug. "Please try to stay calm. I know you aren't looking forward to this, but it will be fine. We've got this, okay?"

He silently nodded.

"I'm going to get my coat. Maybe Mattie went to say goodbye to Penny."

"I just left Penny, but I'll go check."

They parted ways and Sebastian walked down the hall, back toward the sitting room. The library door was ajar and he caught a glimpse of his daughter on the telephone. Opening the door and stepping inside, he said, "Martha, who are you ringing?"

"I'm calling Uncle Alistair, Daddy."

"Where in God's name did you get his phone number?"

"He gave it to me," she said, holding up the calling card.

"Mattie, I don't…" he never had the chance to finish his sentence.

"Hello, Uncle Alistair, it's Mattie." The child listened in response. When it was her turn to speak again, she said, "Daddy and Mummy and I are going to the castle for the weekend. Aunt Penny will be all alone. I think you should come here for tea." Mattie was silent once more while Alistair responded. "She won't mind. She's lonely. Please say you'll come visit." Obviously getting the answer she wanted to hear, Mattie smiled. "Thank you, Uncle Alistair." Then she rang off.

"Martha Katherine Irons, you did not just invite Alistair to tea with Penny." In that moment, Sebastian wasn't sure if he should be angry or pleased with his daughter.

"Yes, I did, Daddy. He said he would be happy to keep Aunt Penny company."

"Fine. Now if you want to go the castle, I'm leaving *now*."

With that, Mattie hopped down from the chair and ran to get her coat.

Soon they were on their way, driving to the country. Traffic was heavier than anticipated. Sebastian's day was not starting out the way he had planned. He glanced over at Tess. "Ask our daughter what she did before we left the house today."

Tess turned around in her seat looked at Mattie with expectant eyes.

"I called Uncle Alistair."

"And the palace just put her through?" Tess exclaimed with alarm, looking back at Sebastian.

"She has his personal number."

"Mattie, why did you call him?"

"I didn't want Aunt Penny to be alone. She's so sad. I can tell Uncle Alistair likes her. He'll make sure she eats while I'm gone."

"Oh, Mattie," Tess repeated, this time her voice soft and caring. "That was a lovely thing to do."

"Only problem is Pen doesn't know Alistair will be showing up on her doorstep," Sebastian explained.

"It's a surprise!" Mattie exclaimed.

Tess reached over and put her hand on top of Sebastian's. "They do seem to be getting along well since the funeral. Alistair has been very kind to Penny."

"I know," he muttered.

"You have enough to worry about. This shouldn't be added to the list. They are adults, Bas."

"Yes, darling," he acquiesced.

The family exited their SUV. The butler greeted them upon arrival at Sutton Castle with a dozen staff in tow. "My Lord and Lady," he said with a slight bow of his head.

"Smyth, nice to see you again," Sebastian greeted, being polite as possible, trying not to show his nerves. He entered the castle first, with Tess and Mattie at his side. Smyth followed next. "My Lord, we've prepared a light luncheon if you would like to eat after you freshen up."

Sebastian looked at Tess.

"Thank you, Smyth. That was very thoughtful," she said, her smile warm and caring.

"I'd like to meet with you in the library at two o'clock to discuss the household," Sebastian said to Smyth.

"Yes, my Lord."

"Thank you. Carry on."

The family walked up the staircase and headed to their rooms. "Daddy, can I have a bigger room?"

"I thought you liked the nursery."

"I'm not a baby anymore. I'm almost five."

"Yes, love, you can choose another room—later, after I've had a chance to speak with Symth." He glanced at Tess. "Would you like a new room, too?"

"I'd like your old room back. It has sentimental value," she said, a smile creeping onto her face. "I like that bed and the shower," she whispered in his ear so Mattie couldn't hear.

Finally, Sebastian smiled too. "I think that's a brilliant idea."

It took an hour to go over the books and expenses, two hours to tour the house and grounds, meeting the staff as they went along. Countless questions were asked by both Sebastian and Tess, which Smyth patiently answered. Thankfully, the stable hand offered his time to take Mattie riding on her pony to keep her occupied so her parents could tend to the business at hand.

Arrangements were made for the family to take over new rooms and Lady Irons' living quarters were discussed.

"I am exhausted," Sebastian announced as he sank into the mattress of his old bed, late that night. Surprisingly, everything had remained the way he had left it all those years ago when he had been banished from the castle. How ironic that he was back as its owner.

"I never knew running a place like this was so involved," Tess agreed, slipping under the covers next to him. "You were amazing today—so confident and businesslike. I'm so proud of you, Bas."

"This is my job now," he shrugged.

"Do you think you'll like it?"

"I don't know, but these people depend on me. I can't let them down." Staring up at the ceiling, he let out a slow breath. "This place is so big. We don't need the whole castle. Maybe we can shut some of it down to help with the cost."

"What if we took one of the wings and set it up with paintings and antiques and opened it to the public, like a museum? Or maybe we could rent the grounds out for events and weddings," Tess suggested.

Sebastian chuckled. "Your mind is at it already. They are both excellent ideas. Let's think about it and talk to Smyth in the morning." A comfortable silence passed between them as they cuddled.

"Sooooo...I have some big news," Tess announced, looking up at her husband.

"Yes?" he hesitantly asked as panic spread through his body.

"Why did you say it like that?"

"The last time you started a conversation like that, you asked me to move to London. We've only been here six months. I can't move again so soon—not now."

"We're not moving," she said to dispel his fear. "Well, maybe we are," she quickly added.

"Darling, I'm too tired to follow your train of thought. Please just spit it out."

"I've decided to leave the AP and work as a freelance journalist. I've made so many contacts, and that interview with Alistair was just the boost I needed to gain some respectability in the industry."

"Why would you do that? You love your job."

"I love you more. I meant it when I said I missed spending time with you and Mattie. If I do this, I can spend more time with you and help you run this place. We could live here full time. I'm sure there are some good schools out here that Mattie can attend."

"There are a lot of ghosts inside these walls."

"But there are good memories, too."

"You really want to live here full time?"

"Why not? We can make new memories—good ones."

Sebastian looked at his wife. He couldn't process what she was saying quickly enough. She wanted to give up her dream job for him. Gobsmacked, he sputtered, "I…I…You'd give it all up for me?"

"I'm not giving anything up, Bas. I think I'm gaining a lot more than I'm letting go. What do you say?"

"Yes," he said, breathing a sigh of relief. "Yes, yes, yes," he repeated in between tiny kisses he planted all over her face.

Tess giggled. "You don't seem so exhausted anymore."

"Got my second wind," he replied in a sexy, playful voice.

"Good, because I was thinking now that we'll be here, spending more time together…" she hesitated to finish the sentence.

Sebastian arched his brow, "You were thinking?"

"Let's have another baby."

The words were music to his ears. Grinning from ear to ear like the fool in love that he was, he kissed her again. "Are you sure?"

Tess nodded. "I know I didn't handle the first time so well, but now I'm prepared. I want this for us. I'll do a better job this time," she declared, serious and resolute.

His spirit soared. She wanted another child. He was the happiest man on earth in that moment. All the stress and anxiety he'd felt earlier in the day evaporated. "I would love to make another baby with you. In fact, we can start now."

# Epilogue - Christmas 1992

Mattie raced down the tiled hall on a red scooter she had received from Santa for Christmas. Sebastian stepped in her path. "Whoa, no racing in the house. You'll break something."

"Daddy!"

"We have guests."

She let out a heavy sigh and perched the scooter against the wall. One of the servants quickly removed it on the spot. Mattie took Sebastian's hand and they walked back to the sitting room where everyone was gathered.

The room held a seven-foot spruce decorated with antique decorations and white fairy lights. The yule log blazed in the fireplace. The mantel was draped with fragrant boughs and holly berries. His daughter's open presents were strewn under the tree.

Mattie walked over to join Grandmom Kate, Henry, and Alice, who were sitting on the sofa having a convivial conversation. Sigourney, Victoria, Martin, and Colette were enjoying a fruitcake. Penny and Alistair stood close together, locked in a private conversation. They only had eyes for each other, muting the lively chaos around them. Lastly, he gazed upon his wife, Tess. She sat back in a comfy chair, the matriarch of Sutton Castle, cradling their newborn son.

"How's William?" he asked, stroking the thin wisp of hair on the infant's head.

"He sleeps like me—hasn't stirred one bit."

"This is madness," he said in a low voice, watching everyone.

"I like to think of it as controlled chaos," Tess grinned. "I think I might write a book about all this one day."

Curious, he asked, "What will you call it?"

"'Love's Great Adventure' has a nice ring to it. I've had the most amazing life with you. I can't wait to see what happens next."

"You don't long for a simpler life?"

"No. I've loved every minute of this crazy journey with you, Sebastian. I wouldn't change a single thing. I love this life."

# Acknowledgements

Editor: Amy Jackson.
Cover Design by Melyssa Winchester
Stock Photo by Yoko Photo Studios
Paperback Cover Design by Addison Kline

My journey as a writer has been an adventure. I want to thank my wonderful author friends: Melyssa Winchester, Ryan Ringbloom, Lisa Suzanne, and Katherine Rhodes and N.M Silber. Your support and advice is treasured.

I can't do this alone, so mega thanks to my street team—Theresa's VIPs: Tracy, Jordan, Jenn, Candice, Wendy, Julie, Teresa, Terri, Lynne and Maggie.

Bloggers, without you my books wouldn't reach the masses. Special thanks to: Cruising Susan Book Reviews, Stephanie's Book Reports, YA Book Madness, Twin Opinions, Romance Obsessed Book Blog, Ropin Romance, Dark Novella, Eskimo Princess Book Reviews, Be My Book Boyfriend, and Books and Beyond Fifty Shades.

Extra special thanks to Tracy Smith Comerford. Your enthusiasm, dedication and hard work is never forgotten and appreciated more than you know!

# About the Author

Theresa Troutman lives in Pennsylvania with her husband and their crazy dog, Niko. She loves reading, theatre, traveling.

Connect with Theresa:

https://www.facebook.com/theresa.troutman.author
Twitter: @ theresatroutman
website: http://theresatroutman.wix.com/theresa-troutman
https://plus.google.com/u/0/+TheresaTroutman
http://www.pinterest.com/theresa4503/

# Other titles by Theresa Troutman

My Secret Summer

A Special Connection

**Love's Great Adventure Series:**

Life's What You Make It

Love This Life

London Loves